Hold Up the Head of Holofernes

Books by Carol Bonomo Albright

AS AUTHOR:

My Greenwich Village and the Italian American Community (2009)

Padri: tre memoir italo americani, with Ned Balbo and Edvige Giunta (2009)

AS EDITOR:

Italian American Autobiographies (1993)

AS CO-EDITOR:

American Woman, Italian Style: Italian Americana's Best Writings on Women (2011)

Wild Dreams: The Best of Italian Americana (2008)

Republican Ideals in the Selected Literary Works of Italian-American Joseph Rocchietti, 1835–1845 (2004)

Italian Immigrants Go West: The Impact of Locale on Ethnicity (2003)

Hold Up the Head of Holofernes

Carol Bonomo Albright

Tough Poets Press
Arlington, Massachusetts

Copyright © 2022 by Carol Bonomo Albright

All rights reserved including the right to reproduce
this book or parts thereof in any form.

Front cover artwork: Detail from *Susanna and the Elders* (1610)
by Artemisia Gentileschi

Back cover artwork: *Self-Portrait as the Allegory of Painting* (1630)
by Artemisia Gentileschi

ISBN 979-8-218-02500-7

Tough Poets Press
Arlington, Massachusetts 02476
U.S.A.

www.toughpoets.com

With much love for my grandchildren,
better by the half dozen;
and to Christine Palamidessi
and Gwen Romagnoli for their
encouragement and unerring eye.

"It says a lot about Carol Bonomo Albright's skill that in this novel about three women in three very different historical epochs, ward politics in 1970s Rhode Island becomes as compelling as Resistance activity in WWII Italy and sexual politics in 17th-century Rome. An impressive fictional debut from one of the great champions of contemporary Italian American writing."
— ANTHONY GIARDINA, AUTHOR OF *NORUMBEGA PARK*

"An admirable effort to interweave, across time and space, the experiences of three women who, having suffered the violation of their bodies, seek a medium—from artistic to legislative—to express the outrage and injustice that persist to this day. The structure of the novel propels the reader forward effortlessly."
— ELVIRA G. DI FABIO, PH.D., HARVARD UNIVERSITY

"The distinction between past, present and future is only a stubbornly persistent illusion."
ALBERT EINSTEIN

LUISA

Rome, December 1943

Luisa stopped pedaling. Her heart was pounding; her breath came in short bursts. She had just biked halfway across Rome. She tried to collect herself, pretending to fiddle with something on her bike chain, all the while keeping a surreptitious eye on the German soldier. He was planted at the intersection a block ahead of her, standing sideways in the narrow street. What was he doing? He was young and had a strong profile. Would she be able to distract him from what was in her laundry basket besides laundry?

This was her first foray as a *staffetta*, a courier for the Resistance. They had given her the four attached nails, which partisans laid on the street to flatten the tires of the Germans' cars. The partisans thought that this was a safe first delivery for her to make. If she were caught, she hoped the repercussions wouldn't be extreme. Flat tires, caused by partisans' nails, were common. Some of the Germans even *almost* laughed it off, as if such an inconvenience would stop them for very long from getting where they were going. *Almost* was the word that Luisa stressed as she thought about what she should do. *Almost laughed it off*, she thought, fiddling with her shoe, tightening the laces. She decided it would look more suspicious if she turned the bike around and retraced her path. How had she gotten herself into this situation? She trembled slightly from the cold or fear—she wasn't sure which—but then she shook her head clear.

For a moment, she thought about what her brother Matteo had said about how the Germans would lord it over the Italians, harm the Jews, intimidate them whenever they felt like having fun, take over the best places to live, the best food to eat. Italy was already starving, drinking an ersatz coffee of chicory—a vile, bitter plant—and they hadn't seen a piece of meat for she couldn't remember how long. Forget about sugar.

Leaning on her bike, Luisa unbuttoned her coat to help her stay cool. She flattened her skirt and smoothed down her red sweater. Her breathing was beginning to return to normal. She patted down her light brown hair and felt the laundry in the basket. Thankfully she couldn't feel the nail instrument. She started pedaling again. As she rode nearer to the soldier, she could hear him talking to someone. His German sounded guttural to her. Its sounds weren't the musical ones of the Italian she was used to.

"Halt," he turned towards her. He had been talking to another Italian, a short man with curly black hair.

The soldier moved towards her. The Italian took advantage of this and started walking away. "Halt," the German hollered at him. The man stopped in mid-stride and looked at the soldier. The German stared back, looked at Luisa, and then shooed the Italian away with his right hand. The man scurried off.

"*Fräulein*," he began, "are you taking a bike ride?" Luisa was surprised. His Italian was quite good.

"Not exactly. I'm delivering laundry that my mother does for other people." She gave the German a big smile.

He smiled back. "But you're not wearing gloves. Aren't your hands cold?

"I'm in a hurry because my mother's customer is waiting for her sheets." He pushed down on the laundry in the basket. Luisa froze.

"So, you're good to your mother, eh?" He gave the basket a nudge.

Luisa stared at him, but stammered, "I do try to help her. We must all help each other, don't you think?"

He chuckled. "Definitely. We should all help each other, *Fraulein*. You'd help me, wouldn't you?"

Luisa thought quickly. She made her most tinkly laugh and

started off on her bike. "It was nice talking to you," she called. "I must get going. My mother's customer is waiting for this delivery."

"*Auf Wiedersehen, Fraulein.*"

Luisa pedaled for all she was worth. She couldn't get away from that man fast enough. As if he'd ever help anyone. She was shivering from fear. This time she was certain that it wasn't from the cold. When he touched the laundry, she had all she could do not to react. She now realized what it was she had gotten herself into. She pedaled at a steady rhythm and as she pedaled, she became more relaxed. She began to appreciate that she had handled herself well. As a matter of fact, she was beginning to feel proud of herself. She had stayed outwardly calm and had even made her getaway appear the normal thing to do. Yes, this courier thing was going to work for her—and for the partisans. She buttoned up her coat and made her delivery. Then she went home.

Giulia, Luisa's mother, was stooped over the kitchen counter, making pasta with a little real flour and some other ingredients that Luisa happily remained ignorant of. Italians had taken to substituting all sorts of things for the ingredients they couldn't buy, not even on the black market. Sawdust baked in bread was the worst.

Her mother pulled a handful of sage leaves she had grown in a pot and fried them in a little oil. When the homemade pasta was cooked, she drained it, added a little oil and the sage—how she hungered for lots and lots of olive oil, or better yet for this dish, butter—and served herself and Luisa.

"So how was your day? What were you up to?" she asked.

"Oh, I went for a bike ride. I thought I might see something that I wanted to take a photo of, but nothing seemed to work."

"Well, there'll be other days and other opportunities," Giulia reassured her. Luisa didn't like lying to her mother, but secrecy as to what she was doing was of paramount importance. This had been made very clear to her. Luisa understood and had no trouble going along with it.

ARTEMISIA

Rome, Gentileschi's Studio, early 1600s

When I was five years old, Father started me drawing. He had me draw a bird. I shaped the head carefully with its little beak curved down, then started on the body. I drew it in flight with one wing pointed down and the other up, for that was how I often observed birds as they launched themselves into the azure sky, so graceful and free from the earth weighing them down.

Father saw my talent and that I was better than my two brothers who, frankly, had no talent at all. Father brought me into his studio. He was a hard and harsh taskmaster. But I didn't mind. I loved the smell of the pigments; turpentine, not so much. Slowly at age ten, I began to mix his colors, pressing down as hard as I could, pulverizing the pigments on the cool marble slab: vermilion, ultramarine, yellow-gold, cinnabar. I loved every minute of it. I watched Father and his workmen go about their daily chores, using an undercoat to heighten the effect of their final painting, capturing the shape of a person's face, the shadows on their skin, the robes flowing around their bodies.

Another five years and I was drawing and painting similar things. But I noticed that, in his paintings, Father idealized women. They never looked like the women I saw every day: women who went to the market, who cleaned and cooked for others. No strong arms to crash the bed linens down on the rocks as they did the laundry. No sweat on their brow. No hurried footsteps as they rushed back from buying food for the family. Little by little, I began to draw and paint the real women I saw and the women I heard about.

Before Mamma died in childbirth when I was twelve—the baby died too—she told me stories. How I missed Mamma! My heart cried for her. Hers was an absence that would never be filled for me. I grieved and grieved for her until I had no tears left. The house became quiet, too quiet. It was no longer filled with her lightness against Father's hardness. Love no longer filled the rooms and no grace pervaded the air. No one to swirl me around in the air by my arms for no reason, except for happiness in my existence. Now I too felt weighed down by the earth.

To bring her back, I told myself the same stories she had told me. About strong, virtuous women from the Bible: Susanna, and Judith, and Jael. And other women too: Cleopatra and Corisca. I told myself these stories over and over until I started painting them, thinking of how Mamma told me the stories. Not only of what happened to them, but of how Mamma painted a picture for me of the character of these women: they were strong women, faithful to what they believed in, no matter what the consequences; they were courageous women who told the truth of a situation even when surrounded by liars. I think Mamma wanted me to have those virtues, because she saw my talent and suspected it would be hard for me as a woman painter in a man's world.

Italy was a man's world then, as all the world was and still is today. I couldn't initiate anything—not even so much as spending money. Father had to be the one to institute an action for me.

Already some of the workmen in his studio were constantly at me, making vulgar remarks, asking if I was a virgin. I put my head down and continued with my work, dismissing their ignorant comments.

Instead of those women Father painted, who looked way too frail to me—even Father's friend, the great Caravaggio, painted a meek Judith, in my opinion—I painted women strong in body and soul, like the *Woman Playing a Lute*. I painted her heft. She's no dainty little thing with graceful robes flowing around her. Rather they're the straight robes of a woman practicing her art. Her sleeves are rumpled. She's solid. Her arms are strong. Her feet are planted on the ground. She knows how life can beat her down, but she'll stand firm. She wears a gold and brown robe, the brown suggesting her earthiness. Even though I'd placed her in a meditative mood, her strength is apparent. I feel that strength too. Does she get it from me or do I get it from her? I wonder.

If I were to paint *Susanna and the Elders* today, I would make her less slender and sinewy than the first Susanna I painted in 1610. I think I was still under Father's sway of more acquiescent figures of women. Although I showed her distress by furrowing her brow and making the twist of her body go one way and her arms the other—a complex pose, to say the least—I wanted to show her outrage at the two men leaning over her. I made the men look like respectable members of the community. They're often the ones who want to force illicit relations upon women because they know, as "outstanding" citizens, they're the ones who will be believed, or, at least, get away with such acts. One stretches out his arm to touch her hair with his hand, threatening to make up stories about her lack of virtue while the other one puts his finger over his lips to urge silence and acquiescence upon her.

Of course, it wouldn't have been wise for Susanna to show her outrage. She had to placate the men in the hopes of their going away and forgetting the whole incident. But we know that wasn't to be. So, I did indeed paint another version of *Susanna and the Elders*, where she's more agitated. Her eyes are cast upwards in distress. She clutches her cloak to hide her nakedness. Her feet are in a fountain, the water a symbol of her purity. This time the character of the leering men is shown for what it is in the lurid expressions on their faces. And then there's the suggestion of the landscape behind her with its dark clouds to show how the world weighs women down to the earth. No easy task for us to fly above it all.

But that painting was made after . . . after the day that I'll never forget. That day damaged the core of my heart with a deep wound. It almost broke my heart—except for what I did afterwards to heal it. But maybe it never healed; at best, I tried to put it behind me and carry on with life, painting out my sorrow, rage, and observations about women and men. The paintings burst out of me. It was as if something else controlled me. Would whatever controlled me be helpful to my painting? I didn't know but I would follow the force of this unnamed energy. I would look forward.

MADDIE

Providence, Rhode Island, June 1978

Having been active in community organizations, Maddie had been offered the opportunity to run for political office. Not that it was much of an opportunity. The party wanted her to run against the senate minority leader, because it needed someone to cover that spot. No one had volunteered to challenge the office holder. Why should they? The incumbent was popular as a voice against one-party rule, Maddie had to admit.

Without a candidate for that spot, there'd be no one to walk the district as a way to get out the vote. Maddie deliberated about the offer. At the least, she'd learn something and at the same time she'd be able to talk about women's issues to voters. The Equal Rights Amendment was making the rounds for constitutional ratification and Maddie found nothing objectionable in it. She couldn't understand what all the fuss was about. All it wanted was equal rights for women. Was that so absurd? Still, she needed to reread the document carefully. Some working women were against it because it took away some special protections they had, as women, in the workplace.

Women's issues, Maddie mused. She was of the generation that felt a woman's main role was to make a home for her family and support her husband. But that hadn't worked for her. Bob and Maddie divorced after a decade and a half of marriage. It had become a rocky relationship midway through their time together. He was obsessed with his career. She was busy taking care of the children, both now away at college, and teaching art history at a nearby community college. They had had good times and bad times.

Now she had more time to delve into artists whose works she was less familiar with, namely two Italian women artists: Sofonisba Anguissola in the sixteenth century and Artemisia Gentileschi from the seventeenth. She was particularly struck by Artemisia Gentileschi's paintings, so strong in their defiance. Artemisia's story, and what happened to her, particularly struck Maddie.

She enjoyed her time alone, the peacefulness of it, doing what she wanted when she wanted. Everything was a trade-off, she knew, and she had risen to the occasion. She had lots of friends and didn't find being alone a great challenge. Weekends were filled with activities that her younger colleagues initiated. They were young enough that life hadn't touched them yet, so their optimism made them cheerful company. But she had to admit that she was looking for a new challenge. Would running for office be that challenge?

Maddie now sat in her neighbor Beatrice's living room, her house just a block away from hers. Beatrice was of Portuguese descent and was active in the bilingual education movement that Portuguese activists in the state were pushing. Their thinking was that Portuguese immigrant students wouldn't fall behind in history, math and science classes if they learned the material in their native language instead of sitting through lessons in English they couldn't understand. Those who opposed that point of view worried that the students wouldn't learn English. A middle ground seemed reasonable to Maddie, where some classes, such as math and science with their complex material, were taught in Portuguese and others in English.

The Portuguese had settled in New Bedford in the first half of the nineteenth century. They were mainly from the Azores, where they were engaged in the whaling industry. After the industry brought them to the shores of New Bedford, some began to stay in the town to practice whaling there. For them the call to "Go West, young man, go West" meant spreading west to Fall River and eventually north to Providence.

Beatrice and her husband were donors to politicians who supported such a language program so she came to have some influence in the party. Alongside Beatrice in her well-appointed living room sat the state representative from the district.

"So, what do you think? Are you up for it?" Beatrice leaned towards Maddie, eager for an answer.

"If it's all right with you, I'd like some time to think about it and I'll let you know. I'm invited to a barbecue tonight so I won't really consider my decision until tomorrow."

"Of course," Beatrice said.

Maddie believed this *was* the challenge she was looking for. A recent meeting of her consciousness-raising group had made her think about a woman's place in society. Some of the women in her group were extremely accomplished, but not valued commensurate with their abilities. One, who was the head of Rhode Island's League of Women Voters, went on archeological digs every summer to exotic locales around the world. Another was an accomplished violinist who performed with a group that played on antique Renaissance instruments. They were invited every winter to play at the State House. Another was an extremely gifted artist, making needlepoints of her original and often witty designs. The art establishment didn't take such "women's handiwork" seriously while the women themselves were well aware of their very serious accomplishments.

Running for office would be a steppingstone for leveling the field for women. Maddie remembered that less than twenty years ago, her sister-in-law had been fired from her job for being pregnant. Equal pay for equal work was a basic issue. Maddie's friend, who taught in a private school, told her that the men earned more than the women. Would society stop seeing men as the "bread winners" and therefore more worthy of employment than women? Would they be hired on the basis of their resumés and not on the basis of their gender? Would men continue to speak over a woman without *listening* to what she was saying? Maddie viewed women's equal place in society not as a "woman's issue," but rather a matter of justice. After all, she mused, wasn't it?

Maddie got ready to walk her district. She chuckled as she thought about the barbecue she had attended two weeks ago. When she told some of the couples there that she had been invited to run for the state senate in her district, the men practically drooled over her opportunity. Their reaction had put aside any reservations she had about running. They considered it a plum to be invited into the dominant party in the state. Maddie could only conclude that there were benefits to being in the party's debt. Hey, this was Rhode Island, where petty corruption was a way of life. Being the smallest state in the union, Rhode Island thought small too: no corruption on a grand scale, just a thousand dollars here and a thousand there. Or a favor done for nothing for someone who might be of help to you down the line.

When Beatrice took her on a courtesy call to the Speaker of the House, he regretted that she didn't have a more WASPy last name. He said it would have helped her candidacy. Maddie was surprised by this since the incumbent mayor was Italian-American, his opponent Irish-American, and the attorney general Jewish. On the federal level, it's true, Maddie thought, Rhode Islanders seemed to go for WASPs, but she was running on the state level. She stayed silent and nursed the brandy the speaker offered her. Not being a drinker at 11:30 in the morning, she had started to refuse the drink, but Beatrice caught her eye and nodded to suggest that she accept it.

Maddie was learning that pragmatism governed all: one state official confided to her that he was a Democrat at the state level but voted Republican in federal elections to protect his financial interests. Maddie already had had an offer of money for her campaign from two developers who were having trouble getting their latest project approved.

She had refused out of principle. She wasn't so hungry for donations that she'd put herself into a difficult situation. It didn't cost much to run in Rhode Island. A candidate didn't need to raise an enormous amount of money. Everyone was eager to be your campaign manager, treasurer, etc., gratis, plus the state didn't make use of television ads. The most they did was a newspaper ad or two, if they even did that. They practiced old time politics, putting up signs on lawns—that sort of thing. Some key friends and supporters had donated enough for her to have campaign literature printed as well as enough money to do a small mailing, which volunteers addressed. Volunteers also held coffees, a method introduced by JFK and followed ever since, that informally brought together the candidate with potential voters.

Maddie herself knew someone who ran a widely circulated neighborhood paper. He did a story on her with her photo included. If she walked her district and got her bumper stickers on cars, she reasoned, she would be OK. Maybe not win, but at least make a respectable showing and have some say in future party issues. She initially thought that she'd learn something, but she was thinking in terms of issues. Instead, what she was learning about was how the state operated behind the scenes.

When Maddie delved into Rhode Island history, one thing she learned was that the WASPs hadn't supported education because they sent their kids to private schools to avoid mingling with the great unwashed. This, of course, led to a large segment of the population without the adequate education that modern jobs demanded.

She looked into the mirror one last time, dabbed on a last layer of red lipstick, and started walking her district. It was a compact district of 10,000 people, like all Providence districts, and easily walkable. Well kept-up single family homes with a scattering of two-family ones dominated. They had neatly tended front yards with lawns that a person could tend to herself. She had been walking her district all week after an early supper, talking to constituents about their concerns. If only people complained about something other than potholes, she thought. That was all people seemed to be aware of or interested in. Surely some other issues demanded attention. She, for example, like US Senator Pell, was all for vocational training.

She knocked on the tenth or eleventh door of the night. The house was one of those Revival Tudors that were so popular. They were handsome homes, she thought to herself. When a woman came to the door, Maddie introduced herself and asked about her concerns.

"I'm concerned about education," the woman said. She was tall and angular and wore rimless glasses. Definitely a no-nonsense type.

Maddie was delighted not to have to commiserate about potholes. She addressed the woman's concerns. They were soon into an animated discussion. Then the woman invited Maddie inside.

"As much as I'd like to sit a while, I need to keep going. I've set myself the task of walking five blocks of my district tonight and I have a way to go yet. But I'll come back another time and we can continue our conversation."

The woman understood. They talked some more, agreeing on some things, agreeing to disagree on others. Maddie told the woman how much she enjoyed talking to her, handed her campaign literature, and then continued on her rounds. More pothole complaints, no doubt.

Local politicians paid attention to potholes. The mayor was known for doing so. He covered streets with blacktop during election years. Some streets became so highly layered that they almost reached the curb. Obviously, the mayor knew what was important to people. Maddie would have a thing or two to learn.

LUISA

Rome, December 1943

During World War I, Luisa's mother Giulia had been about her age now. She used to tell Luisa and her brother stories about that time. She made them sound as if she had been there, presenting scenes in the Alps she had merely heard about.

She didn't talk about the wet, cold trenches the men sat in day after day. That was too mundane a story, having been told over and over again. Instead, she told her two children about how the donkeys, who accompanied soldiers over the Alps, would strain to scale the steep inclines. Even though donkeys were used for heavy work, Alpine crags were another matter: sharp and vertical, covered with icy snow, they made the ascent even more difficult. The lessening of oxygen at that altitude was another problem. But the soldiers, their icy hands almost frozen over their ropes, dragged their donkeys over the peaks to reach their destinations. After all, what choice did they have?

She described the peaceful villages nestled in the valleys at the foot of the Alps, lush with green grass, brilliant in the sunlight. The white cottages, quiet in their repose, served as contrast against the lush green while, above in the Alps, soldiers skied, tramping on the snow and ice at a steady pace, dreaming of warming by the fireside of one of those cottages.

She remembered hearing about a lone grave being dug—only God knows how in that land of ice—on a flat surface of the Alps and marked by a simple cross. The mate of the soldier who had dug it had died from his injuries. How lonely that must that have been for the survivor, to say nothing of the effort of digging in that landscape. But perhaps a grave hadn't been dug, but rather a marker of stones had been placed over his body.

And then there were the dozens of stretchers of the wounded being borne down the cliffs, the angles so steep that the bodies would have slid off the stretchers and down the mountain had they not been secured. To create some traction, the carriers dug into the snow with careful footsteps.

But Luisa was focused on a different aspect of war. She had made the decision to do what little she could by becoming a partisan courier. Yes, she thought, I actually made a decision. In that way, she could live with herself and look herself in the mirror when the war was over. It was always so hard for her to make any decision, but this time she had to make it right away. The war wouldn't wait for her.

It was hard to think about the war ending. It had taken up so much of her life, from before she went to university. Mussolini had been in power for years and now finally the king had dismissed him. Would Badoglio, the new prime minister, be any better? At least marginally so. On that, she'd really just have to wait and see.

This situation of her being a female courier had all started with her brother. When Italy realized that the Axis was losing the war, they switched sides and had gone over to the Allies. Matteo, now in the disbanded Italian Army, was in hiding. He had joined the partisans, who took him to a house in the countryside, to avoid deportation to a slave labor camp or a German concentration camp. He did what he could for the partisans when he could, going out on missions with them.

Before he left for the safe house, Matteo and Luisa had serious conversations. In their first talk, they were standing in her bedroom at the back of their apartment. The shades were drawn against the night sky. His olive-complexioned face was deadly serious. Instead of his usual slouching posture, he stood ramrod straight.

"Luisa," he begged, "you've got to help the effort to aid our people to stay alive during the German occupation."

"What are you talking about?" she gasped. "Stay alive? What do you think the Nazis will do to us? We were their allies."

"Don't be naïve. What they'll do is what they've done to everyone they've conquered. We *were* their allies. But that's not the reality now. Look what they're already doing to the Jews."

Louisa stared at her brother. She had wanted to be a photographer. Now after having graduated from university, her urge to express herself had only gotten stronger over time. As a little girl, her creativity showed itself in childish ways: she had "woven" baskets out of the thickest paper she could find; she tried drawing, but lacked the talent to show the world around her with any accuracy. As she grew older, she had visited museums and once on a family trip to Florence, she had seen a painting that struck her for so long that her mother had to tap her on the shoulder to move on.

"But Mamma," she whined, "look how real he seems." It was a portrait of a Mr. Bertin by Ingres. "I can see what he's like as a person, just by looking at the painting."

"And what did you decide about him?" her mother asked.

"He's not a nice man and . . ." Luisa hurried on, "he's very satisfied with himself when really he shouldn't be." Such portraits made Luisa come alive. They stimulated her to want to do similar things.

Her mother had looked at her daughter in a new light. She certainly had figured out the character of Mr. Bertin. Later at the museum, Luisa had seen Titian's painting of Charles V with his outsized jaw covered by his beard. Even her mother had to admit that Luisa's interpretation of the king as a dullard was right on the mark.

On that same visit to several cities in Italy, Luisa saw a painting of Judith and her maidservant by Artemisia Gentileschi and of a lute player by the same artist in a Roman gallery. She was bowled over by the paintings and was surprised to see works of a woman artist from the seventeenth century. She had no idea women were doing such accomplished and eye-catching works back then. She lingered over both paintings for a long time. The women's faces and their powerful arms told the whole story. Little did she know at the time that she would have something in common with Artemisia Gentileschi.

"I want to do with photography what these painters have done: show the soul of the person," Luisa had said. Her mother remained silent and thoughtful. At the time, Luisa hadn't thought further than that.

"But what can I do about it?" she asked Matteo. "I'm just a girl who wants to survive this war—in *peace*." She laughed at her little word play and continued, "The Allies will be here soon, I'm sure of it . . . They're already in Salerno . . . and kick the Germans out."

Matteo looked at her thoughtfully. He was surprised at her response. He thought he knew his sister. As a little girl, she had always thought of others. She gave some of her birthday money to charities that helped poor children. But that urge was different from following political acts, something that Luisa hadn't done. How could she make silly jokes during a time like this? He decided to tell her what was going on in Rome at this very moment.

"You're right, Luisa. You're just a girl and I'm just a guy. What can we do? We can do whatever there is to be done. The partisans are looking for girls to be couriers to carry messages and weapons. The Germans won't suspect girls. We disbanded soldiers will hide out and sabotage whatever we can, whenever we can. You'd be surprised to learn what we ordinary people are doing—not that we know who's involved. That's the first rule. No one knows of anyone else—except for their handler and their team if they have one—so that if one is captured, they can't give the Germans any information about a lot of others."

Luisa fell back onto her bed. She was shocked. She hadn't expected to hear Matteo say these things. Although she was a university graduate, she had taken courses to become an elementary school teacher. Mussolini thought that was one of the jobs that women should do—nothing in the professions or higher education. This vocation wasn't Luisa's first choice but she had gone along with it. Then, too, she thought she'd be able to do her photography on the side while she taught. But in point of fact, not being a card-carrying Fascist, she hadn't been able to find a teaching job.

Luisa suddenly remembered a book, published in the United States, that her American relatives had sent. The series contained stories about children from around the world. They thought the family would enjoy reading one of the stories, which was about Italy. It told of two children, Lucia and Beppo. When Lucia grew up, she wanted to be a mother of many Fascist babies and Beppo wanted to become a soldier for Mussolini's empire. Beppo says he'll do anything the Duce tells him to do "without asking why; just because he says a Fascist should do it." At the time, she hadn't really focused on it and wrote a thank you letter to her Calabrian-American relatives for thinking of her. Now she thought of the story as despicable. Not only were the roles of the children demeaning, but in October of 1935, Mussolini had invaded Ethiopia. The saving grace for the publishing company was that the book was written and published before that invasion, but to portray Mussolini's Italy so positively went against the grain. Mussolini had been making war-like statements for a long time. It seemed everyone was on to Mussolini, but no one was objecting.

The war had changed no one and everyone. It certainly changed Matteo. Before, he was like a crazy person: when their father died, he took on the responsibility of policing her honor as a woman. Certainly, her father hadn't gone to the lengths that he had. If Matteo discovered that she was out of the house, on a *passegiatta* walking with her girlfriends, Matteo chased after her, shouting like a crazy man to get back into the house. He had taken on his new role as the man of the house with an extreme diligence. It was unnerving to Luisa, but she couldn't think of any way to stop him. Her girlfriends tried to talk to him, but it was useless. Even Antonio, her brother's best friend, had talked to him to no avail. Luisa was well aware that boys could get out of hand, but a walk on the main street of their neighborhood was hardly a compromising situation.

And then the war came and Matteo's service in the Italian Army.

He must have seen things that changed him. Not that he talked about it with either her or her mother, but he was a different person. Luisa's *honor* no longer concerned him to the extent it had before, if at all. Thank God, Luisa thought. Strangely, war had made him gentler, more compassionate and able to see other people's points of view. He never talked about what he saw, but Luisa felt sure that what he had seen had affected him deeply. He had become passionate about stopping the Germans at all costs, even to the extent of urging Luisa to work with the partisans.

Another time, he had apologized to her for his past behavior. "Luisa," he sputtered, "I'm sorry for how crazy I treated you after Papa died. I thought that now that I was the head of the household, I needed to exert my authority over you. I was so foolish. Papa never would have treated you like that. But I missed having him around to guide me. I went off the deep end. I felt torn up and guilty."

"What did you feel guilty about?" Luisa asked in astonishment. She wanted to understand.

"I didn't think I was doing enough. Later on, even though I gave Mamma most of my pay—it wasn't much—I felt guilty because I couldn't *be* Papa. I couldn't do it all, but I *could* oversee you."

"Oh, Matteo, I should have understood what you were going through when Papa died, but I was in mourning for him too." She stayed silent, thinking back on all Matteo had put her through. His screaming at her in the streets was humiliating. It made her appear to be a loose woman, which was the farthest thing from the truth. She wanted to yell at him and ask how he could have done that. At the same time, she recognized that their father's death had affected them both. Besides that, he *was* a different person now. The war had changed him. His demeanor was much quieter, reflective even. He thought first and then acted if he thought action was needed. She took a breath and rose to her better self.

"Of course, I forgive you. You're my brother and I'll always love you." Thinking back to that time, Luisa's eyes teared up. She shook her head. She had to think about what Matteo was telling her now.

She had to make a decision.

Making decisions was not her forte. As a little girl, she found it impossible even to decide which pastry she wanted when at the bakery with her mother. Once her mother couldn't wait for Luisa to decide and she bought both pastries that Luisa was torn between, cut them in half and gave Luisa half of each one. Her mother made sure to tell Luisa that she wouldn't do that again because it would be as if she were rewarding her daughter for being indecisive. But that was a long time ago. After that, her mother helped Luisa in making decisions so that she could become better at making them on her own. But Luisa wondered if she were still the same kind of wishy-washy girl or would she rise to this situation and make a decision?

A few days later on a foray into Trastevere, she had seen for herself the Germans rounding up Jews in the nearby Jewish Ghetto. She had taken her camera with her that day and quickly snapped a photo from across the river. It showed German soldiers shoving a Jewish family into the back of a truck, already crammed with others.

Another German had noticed Luisa and yelled at her, but he lost interest in pursuing her as she raced away on her bike. He had other things to attend to. She felt that the photo she had just taken needed to be done, even if she couldn't say exactly why. It wouldn't stop the Germans from rounding up the Jews, but after the war, it might act as documentation as to what they had been up to.

GIULIA

Rome, December 1943

Luisa's mother thought this current war was ill-conceived, though she never spoke against it outside the house. She considered Mussolini with his jutting chin to be a clown, a dangerous clown. When the Allies finally landed in Italy, she took heart. Maybe, just maybe, this was the beginning of the end. She hoped so. She worried for her children: Matteo on the run, Luisa's life on hold just when she should have been beginning the first phase of her adulthood, working at a job she loved.

Even with Badoglio in power now, Giulia had little hope for the future. No sooner was Badoglio named prime minister, than the next night he and the King abandoned Rome. This action didn't bring a lot of faith or hope in their government to the Italians.

Things had gotten even worse. The Germans now occupied the northern and central parts of the country. Initially, the Nazis had been bad friends and now they were even worse enemies: rude, arrogant and ruthless. She hated having to do errands on the streets of Rome for fear of running into one of them, attracting their attention and inadvertently doing something to upset them.

How did we ever end up on their side, she mused? Mussolini was a child. He thought that by sidling up to Hitler, he'd be in the big league of world leaders. Narcissistic babies was more like what both leaders were. But babies who could, nonetheless, create havoc and misery for millions of people. She didn't want to think about Hitler. He was a madman, pure and simple. Had there ever been a ruler as evil as he? She didn't know enough about history to have the answer to that question.

The Germans had been Italy's enemy in World War I. Was it a good thing to switch sides this time around? Certainly not with the Germans who were hunting down Jews and were now their occupiers. She shuddered, thinking about the Nazis amidst them. She didn't like when Luisa went out riding her bike, but she couldn't keep her daughter in the house all the time. Luisa was going out more and more. She'd have to have a word with her about that. But Luisa was a *testa dura*, hard-headed, as her Calabrian great-grandmother would have said. Giulia would do her best.

She prayed that Matteo, to evade the Nazis, was well hidden in a house in the countryside, but hiding was getting increasingly dangerous. Giulia had heard that many Italian Jews and escaped prisoners of war were in hiding in the countryside. She nurtured a foolish hope, she knew, that Matteo was hiding in the Alpine village where his paternal grandparents lived and with whom the family had stayed during vacations. Yet, how long would it be before the Nazis started poking around in those villages and finding those in hiding? No place was safe.

The countryside people were taking a big chance hiding Jews, but she understood their motivation. The Jews were their neighbors. They had lived among them for decades, some for centuries after the fifteenth-century Inquisition ousted them from Spain. In many instances, they looked like Italians. You couldn't tell the difference between an Italian and a Jew. They were simply all citizens who attended different buildings of worship. Once the government came out against the Jews, passing those disgraceful racial laws, it only fortified the Italians to help the Jews, because there was a big streak of anarchism among Italians: if the government said to do one thing, the Italians were sure to do the other.

Giulia sighed. She dropped her face into her hands and tried not to solve all the problems of the world. Her biggest problem at the moment was what could she prepare for supper.

MADDIE

Providence, June 1978

Maddie sat in the gray armchair with the curled wooden armrests, staring out her living room window. She was catching her breath for a minute before she started working on her campaign. A weak sun brushed against her cheek, lighting her pale skin. She barely saw what was out there to see: the mock orange shrub, a rose of Sharon bush, a leafy maple, rose bushes, a quince tree, all surrounding a large grassy area.

Seeing the quince tree, the fruit not yet ripe, reminded her of a trip she had taken to Morocco, the last major trip she had taken. She wanted to know more about that part of the world. The desert there amazed her, more even than the desert in Egypt. Maybe because she had ridden a camel in this one. Well, not exactly ridden, she thought. It was more like walking a camel for a short time, but it was long enough to make her legs, and other parts of her body, ache.

She looked forward to the quince maturing. Then she could make the Moroccan dish that she loved so much: chicken with preserved lemon and quince. Thinking of that exotic trip made her think about the Hmong immigrants from Cambodia who helped the United States during the Vietnam war. When the war ended, the United States government settled some in Rhode Island. The group who came had been a success story. Despite the trauma of war, one of the youngsters became valedictorian of his high school class. The principal, commenting on the event, hoped that the student wouldn't become "American," suggesting that many American students didn't take their studies as seriously, nor work as hard, as he had.

She found her mind drifting back to wars: the Second World War in particular. As a child, she never could imagine what the hardships of war were like. What she remembered was a joke that was being made towards the end: What did Hitler say when he took off his boots? I smell de-feat. She didn't even know if she had gotten the double entendre since she was only about four or five when the war ended. Nonetheless, she loved that joke and remembered it all these many years later.

She remembered her mother taking her to the stores uptown when she heard that nylon stockings were for sale. She'd rush up there, hat on her head—a red one with a jaunty feather—ignoring the blaring of cars' horns as she crossed against the lights to arrive in time. Then, with Maddie in tow, she'd wait in the crowded store in a line for a pair of nylons. Next, she'd leave Maddie on the side, holding her red hat, and get on line again for another pair of stockings. Her disguise was never discovered.

Maddie's mom had a number of disguises, if you could call them that. She was charming outside the home when she wanted to obtain something, but to her own family she could be brusque.

Maddie had never felt any hardship regarding the rationing of food, though she was sure her mother had used her ingenuity and charm to get what the family needed. She was that kind of person. She still continued to bake Toll House cookies, Maddie's favorite. Her mother had many talents.

Another memory she had was of their good friends' son quite a while after returning from the war. But this memory wasn't lighthearted and funny. She was a young teenager by then when they visited. All the while laughing and adding sounds of guns going off, their son told stories about machine-gunning houses indiscriminately as the US Army made its way up the Italian boot. Had enough time gone by that he could now turn the fighting into a comic routine—a routine that he repeated every time he visited?

She never could understand his laughter, but, she reasoned, everyone deals with the stress of war in his own way. He presented the scenes of death as full of life and victories for the army. Strange. As an adult as she thought more about it, she decided that his repeated "laughter routine" was a way for him to dispel the fear he had felt at that time.

He and his father were good-looking men, both more than six feet tall. The father was charming in a corny sort of way and the son was a joker. In his own way, was he competing with his father? Maddie was no psychologist, but she couldn't help but wonder at the son's behavior. Someone else could probably see some connection that she couldn't.

A cloud flashed across the sun, putting her in shadow. Maddie walked to the front of the house to see if her azalea bushes were flowering yet. She sank into the chair on the front porch. Her thoughts wandered again. She shook herself. She had to get moving. She had a campaign to run.

ARTEMISIA

Rome, early 1600s

When Mamma died, Father eventually hired Tuzia to help with the housework and to chaperone me when he was out. I couldn't even go to church without her. At least she was a help when it was time to buy pigments.

"Tuzia," I called. "We need to go to the apothecary for pigments."

"*Si, si,*" she answered in her typical tired voice.

"Why must I always drag you there?" I scolded.

"Ah, Artemisia, I have so much work to do in the studio and at the house and now I have to walk to the apothecary and back? It's too much." She put the palms of her hands on her lower back to stretch out her tired bones. She often complained to me about something or other. I felt sorry for her even though I knew she was exaggerating and hoping for an extra lira or two. But Father was as tight as Tuzia was desirous of more money.

"Don't be like that. When we return from the apothecary, you'll be able to sit down to the nice meal that you are cooking."

She grumbled a bit more, but shuffled along to the apothecary, dragging her feet and carrying a basket for the supplies I was to buy. We trudged along on the stones at a snail's pace on Tuzia's part, at a gallop on mine. I had to wait for her on each and every corner.

"*Buon giorno.*" I greeted Mario who would provide me with the pigments I needed. I barely glanced at him, so anxious was I to bask in the beauty that started right here in this little shop. There were so many luscious colors to choose from. I wanted to buy them all, but we could hardly afford that. There was one blue pigment, ultramarine, so expensive that we could only buy it for special projects. I took my time reveling in all the choices I had, lingering on the gold and vermilion, feasting my eyes on the gem-like greens, reds, and the alabaster white. Not that I really had much choice. Father had ordered me to buy exactly what was needed.

Mario interrupted my reverie. "What can I get you today, little one?"

"Nothing very exciting today, Mario. Some of that brown and black, if you please."

"They're always very useful," he said, ever the salesman.

I remained serene, feasting on all the possibilities. When I was free to paint what I chose, I'd sell my work and be able to buy whatever pigments I needed and wanted. I couldn't wait.

Father retained a teacher for me, Agostino Tassi, a fellow artist with whom he occasionally collaborated. My father was always on the lookout for his main chance and he thought that by having Tassi in the studio, he and I might collaborate with Tassi on his commissions for large paintings, which he received from important people, like bishops and lords. Works of that size always needed many artists to complete the work. One might work on certain figures like angels, another on the sky and so forth.

Father already had a high regard for my professional expertise. I'll give him that. When I was seventeen, he said that I had no peer anywhere in painting. He was sure that my talent would weigh the balance for commissions with Tassi in his favor, always *his* favor, never mind what I might have wanted. As my teacher, Tassi was to instruct me in the finer points of perspective, among other things.

I was to study first perspective in painting: how objects, receding into the background, become smaller until they recede to a vanishing point. I looked forward to learning more from my father's friend because I felt that Father had taught me all that he was capable of.

Perspective, I knew, was a tricky element in painting. I knew a little about perspective in painting scenes, but little about the perspective of men, which, alas, was of a different nature. When I think back on those early lessons, I marvel at my eagerness and my naïveté.

Agostino Tassi was a well-proportioned, slender man with a bushy mustache and a neat goatee, flecked with gray. His brown hair fell straight to his shoulders and his eyes were the color of iron. When he entered father's studio, he seemed to appraise me for a few minutes. Under his stare, I began to move from one foot to another.

"Shall we begin?"

I understood that it wasn't a question. I took my place in front of him and he pointed to one of Father's finished paintings.

"You can see that the perspective is off. The road is all wrong," he declared.

I had observed this myself but felt that I couldn't criticize Father's work, especially to someone who wasn't part of the family. Besides, Tassi was exaggerating. The road was hardly "all wrong." I remained silent. He waited.

"Well, do you see that or not?" he demanded. I nodded my head.

"Was that a yes?" I nodded again.

"You're a quiet one, aren't you?" He paused. I didn't know if he was waiting for a response. We sat in silence.

"All right, let's commence the lesson." With that he started drawing various scenes, some with proper perspective and others not. I waited, growing impatient.

"Which have proper perspective?"

I pointed to the ones I thought were done properly. He turned and looked at me.

"All right. Now we can begin in earnest." And with that he analyzed what was wrong about each of the examples he had drawn of improperly executed perspectives. Next, he set me various perspective problems to solve. I worked slowly and carefully, thinking about the problem connected to each one, before putting charcoal to paper. He turned again to look at me. All this appraisal of me made me uncomfortable. Better that he should concentrate on what he was here for: to teach me more about perspective, rather than this sizing me up. He released me from his gaze and studied my work.

"Well done," he said. I sat back, let out a sigh, and folded my hands.

"We'll continue next Tuesday." And with that he strode out of the studio. I assumed he had accepted me as a student.

"Today we'll work on the undercoat, necessary to enrich the colors to be added, to give them depth. Do you understand?"

Of course I did. I had been doing Father's undercoats for a while now. But I simply nodded.

"Do you have a voice?" he asked. "Please use it."

'Yes, *maestro*," I answered.

He began with instructions on how to build a good undercoat. I followed his directions. Over time he became less brusque. He made a feeble joke every now and then, though humor was not his forte. He gave me a systematic overview of what every painting needed. I was beginning to respect his knowledge if nothing else.

As my chaperone, Tuzia oversaw our sessions in the studio. She brought peas for shelling or some piece of clothing that needed mending. She paid little attention to what was going on in our lessons. As far as she was concerned, even though she disliked the smell of the pigments, it was a good opportunity to sit and catch up on her tasks in a quiet setting.

While I painted, Tassi observed my work. But it was not only my painting that he observed. He observed *me*. I had grown into womanhood and because I was no great beauty, but a comely woman nonetheless, I was intrigued by his attentions. I was learning about what interested men. Not that I encouraged him in any way. I knew what encouragement of a man could mean for a young woman. First and foremost, I wanted to learn what I could about painting from him. I was devoted to my art and didn't want any complications.

I wanted to become a great painter. I'd show the world that women were able to do more than what was expected of them. It seemed so apparent to me that they were the equals of men. I wondered why no one else saw this. Right here in my household, I had my untalented brothers as examples. Not only was I their equal, but as far as painting went, I was superior to them. If I had been sent to study as they were, I could have learned to read and write. But that wasn't thought to be necessary for a girl. Only they would experience the delights of reading Ovid and other authors. Or be able to sign their names beyond using an X for a signature, like me.

Did saying that I was more talented than my brothers make me boastful? I didn't think so. Just as Judith from the Bible knew what she was capable of in murdering Holofernes, the enemy of her people, so too did I know my worth as a painter. Wasn't my ability seen in every canvas I painted? Hadn't Father told me that I had no peer in painting? The strength my women showed impressed him with their reflection of actual women. Didn't Augusto Tassi increasingly praise my work with him?

Why did Romans, as well as the whole of Italy, keep women in one slot? Women had no rights of their own. They were to live their lives as wives and mothers, or, if that wasn't possible, to become nuns. Living in a convent always held for me the specter of being imprisoned. What did they do all day besides pray and sing and tend to their chores? Why couldn't women be wives and mothers and follow their talents at the same time? Did God ordain this? I didn't see how He could have. Or if He had, what kind of a God could He be? Not to be blasphemous, but, to me, He'd be deeply flawed. After all, he had made both Adam *and* Eve.

As one might suspect, our household wasn't deeply religious. We followed the culture of our times, but as far as being pious believers, we would have none of it. So maybe my attitudes could be understood. I was a questioning child and a questioning adult. I waived judgement about such things and mainly concerned myself with my painting. After what happened to me, I should have had a broader perspective.

LUISA

ROME, JANUARY 1944

Luisa was feeling the stress from her work for the partisans. After initiating her into delivering nails, they started using her to relay messages. Then she started carrying weapons to partisans, the most dangerous activity so far. She wasn't happy about that, but she did it. She knew how important such deliveries were. Now, having learned of her photographic ability, they had her taking photos of Jews who needed false papers for passports and other such documents. The Germans believed in documents. They documented everything.

Taking photos was more dangerous: first because she had to go to the safe houses where the Jews were hiding and secondly because Luisa had to bike into the countryside where the Jews were. Who could tell when an enemy soldier would show up on one of the roads or in a village? Or a village neighbor would become suspicious at seeing strangers arriving at a safe house and inform on the family. The turncoat could earn up to 5,000 lire for such information—a fortune.

The partisans had set up a well thought out system of creating false documents. First, a false name was used. As a person's place of residence, they put the name of a city or town that had been thoroughly bombed. Then they chose a street that had been destroyed, so that the town's registry office, which was no longer operational, couldn't be checked against the family's supposed address.

If Luisa were ever stopped while biking through the countryside, she had concocted a story: she was practicing her photography so that after the war, she would be proficient enough to get a job using her photographic skills. She made sure to have some photos of scenery on her film so that if a German soldier demanded the film in her camera, she was covered. If her nerve held, she even thought she might invite the German soldier to have her take his picture. Despite her own experience of loss and loneliness, this partisan work was making her a determined young woman.

The partisans kept the film with the photos on it and they developed it. Then Luisa would be given another role of film. She'd snap some scenes so that if she were stopped upon returning to town, she could use the same cover story.

Today would be particularly difficult. It would be a long session. She had to take photos of a whole family: mother, father, two children, and two grandparents—all the while concerned about the German soldiers coming into the village. Moreover, she wasn't just worried about enemy soldiers. She didn't trust the *carabinieri*, who were an arm of the Italian government, where many Fascists worked. Her fears were beginning to run away with her. She was seeing enemies behind every tree. She had to gain control over herself and take one step at a time.

Luisa rode through the countryside. The tree branches were bare of leaves and covered with frost. She didn't let her guard down as she surveyed the icy beauty of the landscape. Suddenly her head snapped to attention. A train came into view: a long line of boxcars, used to transport cattle. Where were they going—and so many of them?

She continued to stare at the cars and then she saw a hand feebly waving out of a small opening in one of them. Trembling, she fell backwards onto the seat of her bike. She understood what those cars were transporting—Jews. Maybe the Jews she had seen being rounded up in the Ghetto and elsewhere in Rome. Her heart swelled. The train continued on. Luisa's began riding her bike, her pace slowed. The sight of those boxcars stuffed with people had knocked the wind out of her.

Luisa knocked on the door of the farmhouse where the family was hidden. An older gentleman, on the short side with powerful arms, came to the door and asked her what she wanted.

"I was hoping to buy some eggs," she said, as she had been told to answer the question.

"How many do you want?" he answered.

"A half dozen, if you please."

"That's a lot of eggs with a war on."

"Whatever you have then. My mother would like to make a *frittata*."

"I can sell you two. Come in."

His answers, like hers, followed the script she was given. She entered the building. It was a typical farmhouse with two floors and an attic. The ground floor held the living area, dominated by a large kitchen with a fireplace in which a small fire crackled. A slight odor of burning wood rose in the room. Soft drafts drifted through the cracks of the old house, offering some relief from the stuffy air.

The woman of the house was cleaning greens. Luisa had had her fill of greens. Swiss chard and spinach had become the staples of her diet. She wondered if what she called real chickens as opposed to egg-producing ones were on the farm. Her mouth watered as she thought of devouring one.

The second floor held the bedrooms. The Jewish family hid in the attic above. Luisa climbed the steep stairway, winding back on itself, no handrail to aid her as the well-worn steps wobbled beneath her feet. When she opened the door, dust and a stale, musty odor overwhelmed her. She hadn't thought ahead to what conditions would be like in such a situation.

She was shocked by how thin and pale they all looked and how slack the family's skin was. She knew that food was hard to get. She herself had lost weight, but she thought food would be more plentiful in the countryside. Even polenta, which had quickly become the staple food, was in short supply when you had six extra mouths to feed. As for going outside to feel the sun on your skin, that was out of the question. Yet she knew that many Jews now lived under such conditions. And they were the lucky ones.

Luisa greeted the family who responded quietly. They were used to speaking in whispers and moving in socks and on tiptoe so as not to compromise their hosts. You never knew when someone might enter the house and you couldn't be sure of where their sympathies lay.

Luisa could see that the mother and father had been a good-looking couple who now showed nothing but distress on their faces. The father had a long face with regular features and brown eyes. How sad his eyes were. And his face looked haunted. Who wouldn't be after all that they were going through, Luisa thought, as she studied his face?

The mother was of a calmer nature. She looked up from the paper she was reading, removed her glasses, squinted at Luisa and then gave her a faint smile. Her eyes were alert, showing little of her husband's sorrow. Perhaps their situation weighed most heavily on him as the head of the household, feeling inadequate because he couldn't protect his family as he would have liked.

The children seemed more resilient, mirroring their mother's composed demeanor. They looked up from their schoolbooks and greeted Luisa with big smiles. Luisa judged the boy to be about seven or eight and the girl about six—too young to be aware of the great danger they were in. Luisa wished she had a piece of chocolate or some other sweet to give them, but she herself hadn't seen sugar, or any sugared food, since the war started. The grandparents had a look of resignation and fragility about them. They stood next to each other, stooped and weary. They had lived through the first world war.

She positioned each member of the unfortunate family against a black piece of fabric, which the owners of the house had supplied, and near a lamp that had been especially set up for this situation. She quickly snapped photos of the six family members. Only the little girl gave her trouble. She kept moving, but Luisa spoke to her in a whisper, emphasizing how still she must stay. She complied. Luisa left the film in the farmhouse and received a new roll of film. Before she started on her return journey, the woman of the house handed her two eggs.

"In case any German soldiers stop you. And for the *frittata* your mother wants to make." The woman winked at Luisa as she gave her the eggs. "It isn't much, but it's all I can spare under the circumstances."

For a moment, Luisa thought she shouldn't accept the eggs, but the words wouldn't come out of her mouth. She had visions of one of her mother's *frittatas*, dancing in her head. Finally, she said, "I understand and it's more than generous of you. I shouldn't accept these, but frankly my mother and I are starving and I find it impossible to refuse. Thank you so much for all your help." Luisa positioned each egg into a pocket of her coat and quickly biked away from the house. When she judged that she was far enough away to avoid revealing where she had been, she snapped a couple of generic scenes that could be found anywhere. She made sure that the two eggs were secure in her pockets.

By the time Luisa reached home, it was almost curfew time. She entered the apartment that she shared with her mother, wiped her brow, and sat down on a kitchen chair. Her mother stared at her. She knew that Luisa was up to something, but, she reasoned, the less she knew, the better. The Gestapo couldn't squeeze out of you details that you didn't know. Nonetheless, Giulia was worried about her daughter. She viewed her daughter as an innocent and an idealist, a bad combination in wartime.

"You look tired, Luisa."

"I am a bit. I biked farther than I intended."

"You need to be careful about getting back home by curfew."

"I know but at least for my journey I was able to get us two eggs." She pulled them out of her pockets with a flourish and placed them on the kitchen table. It was getting harder and harder to find food even on the black market. Tears came to Giulia's eyes. How silly of me, she thought, to tear up from seeing two eggs, two farm-fresh eggs.

"You're very resourceful, Luisa. Be careful. Be very, very careful. War is no game for the innocent."

GIULIA

Rome, February 1943

Giulia had been hearing more and more stories about what was going on. She read about Hitler's visit to Rome for his grand imperial parade. In newspaper photographs, he looked like he was hallucinating. His soldiers had done the goosestep. It was alarming, to say the least.

She heard stories about what was happening in the countryside. So many Jews were hiding there that a network was set up to keep the Jews informed about what was happening.

She knew that Jewish children could no longer attend school. They were isolated and missed their classmates, who never contacted them for fear of Fascist repercussions. Some Jewish students were hidden in boarding schools run by nuns. The students were so hungry that they ate the crust of the polenta that remained on the pot before it was washed.

One sympathetic vicar would inform the nuns when the Germans would be "visiting" the school so that the nuns could hide the Jewish students. Or a sympathetic doctor would place the Jewish students in quarantine, telling the Germans that they had one or another disease that was contagious. The chicken-livered Germans didn't tarry. They ran out of the room, tripping over each other.

Once when the Germans came to the boarding school, one of the soldiers, Giulia had heard, gave a cookie to one of the Jewish children, who could "pass." She had never seen a cookie in her young life and was afraid to eat it.

So much misery. Giulia didn't know how those in hiding stood it.

She hoped that Matteo suffered less than those tragic children. If he had been lucky enough to land in his grandparents' village in a valley of the Alps, maybe things would be easier there. It was harder to get to, for one thing, but she knew in her heart that she was dreaming a dream that had a million to one chance of occurring. Ah well, she sighed, that's what dreams were made of. They were as insubstantial as air.

She shut the book that she had been holding in her hands but hadn't read. There was no electricity to see the words. She fondled the soft cover of the book, blew out the candle, placed the book on her night table, and tried to sleep.

ARTEMISIA

ROME, EARLY 1600S

Tassi and I developed a rapport. I learned many things from him, most minor points but, in painting, every little thing makes a difference. Two-point perspective was the latest lesson. Two vanishing points were placed on a horizontal line. I was made to understand that it was useful when painting buildings, something I rarely did, but I paid attention anyway. One never knew when such knowledge would be needed.

We also worked on color. I was partial to yellow and a rich gold, which I used often. It lit up a painting, especially when I used Caravaggio's chiaroscuro technique with a dark background. Caravaggio was a friend of Father's. I was a great admirer of his paintings. He encouraged me in my efforts and I appreciated that. As for other colors, I built up the color, black for example, with many colors before adding the black itself, adding a depth to the final effect.

Tuzia continued to sit in on my lessons and to complain about having to walk to the apothecary for pigments and I continued to chide her about her complaints. On one walk there, we ran into a neighbor boy, Giorgio, with a pronounced Adam's apple. He was a little taller than I and had brown hair that curled in soft ringlets. He stopped me to talk.

Tuzia took offense at this and began to berate me. Why, I wondered, didn't she berate Giorgio? He initiated the conversation. I shushed her and continued to talk to Giorgio. He would make a good model for me to practice my drawing of the male body.

There were certain things that would be off limits in my drawing of him, but the musculature of his arms and legs would be visible, and maybe his chest, as well as that dominant Adam's apple. Before Tuzia knew what was happening, I quickly invited him to my studio, the Wednesday next. Then Tuzia and I proceeded to the apothecary.

I was excited beyond belief. Although I had painted men, I had no assurance that my rendering of their anatomy was accurate. When he arrived that Wednesday, I positioned him in the brightest section of my studio, first just standing before me. I took out my drawing pad and commenced. Next, I had him sitting with one leg crossed over the other. Tuzia huffed as she sat there. I ignored her and proceeded to sketch in his Adam's apple.

At my prodding, he removed all the layers of clothing that hid his chest. He preened a bit and liked that I was scrutinizing his torso. I could see his well-developed pectoral muscles as well as his subclavius ones. He and I fell into conversation, but I kept my talking to a businesslike tone. The time slipped away and I was pleased at what I was discovering. Tuzia continued to harumph, something she was expert at doing. I paid her no attention and concentrated on Giorgio. And so passed a very worthwhile day. We made an appointment for another session. I wanted to draw his back as well as pose him in different positions.

I continued to meet with Tassi, but it was my meetings with Giorgio that I was excited about.

MADDIE

PROVIDENCE, JULY 1978

Having finished the preliminary chores connected to her campaign for state senator of her district, hiring a staff, creating campaign literature—one handout of a size that could fit into a business-sized envelope and mailed as well—and continually walking her district, Maddie started on her next activity. She was expected to attend and speak at all rallies that the party held. Public speaking wasn't something she had ever done. She had experience talking in class, of course, but speaking to a much larger group of diverse people, none of whom she knew, as well as seasoned politicians who were running for office at the same time as she, was a different kettle of fish.

The candidates stood in a row while a master of ceremonies tried to whip up the crowd into some kind of enthusiasm, making generic comments about the glory of the party past, the glory of what could be accomplished for them, and the glory of America. This latter appeal to their love of a great country never failed to get voters out of their chairs to cheer.

Maddie had no idea what to say so she threw out a few bromides as well as mentioning her key campaign issues. Her little speech went over with a thud. Then she listened to the seasoned pols who spoke next: all generalities, again appeals to patriotism, and reminders of how the party had helped them before, would never forget their support, and would help them again, all received with wild cheers. She listened and learned, junking mention at future rallies of specific campaign issues.

The rallies were held in diverse sites: school auditoriums, clubs of various sorts—the Portuguese-American club, fishing and hunting clubs—halls of various kinds in accessible locations and large enough to hold a crowd, but not too big to fill.

At one rally, the candidate for mayor initially gave a quiet, meditative speech, which Maddie thought was excellent. At the end of the program, he strode back onto the stage and said his wife had sent him back because he had been too abstract earlier. He needed to say what he would do for the voters. His remarks were couched in general terms but he brought down the house with the usual generic superficialities shouted at them. In this masterful performance, bellowing trumped anything of substance.

Again, Maddie thought about how much she had to learn about rallies and the voters who attended them. They seemed like true believers. This wasn't the sort of discourse she was used to in the classroom, where discussion and reasoned disagreements could be aired. But she was confident that she could learn to do "political speak."

After the rally, she met ragtag followers one on one and regular donors as well as old time pols who came out to relive their glory days. One old-timer, poorly shaven and leaning on a cane, told her with pride how they, meaning the party leaders, finagled a win for one state representative. From polling, they knew that the race in his district was extremely close so on election day they found the names of three recently deceased men still on the voting rolls—and he was very specific about the number three—and sent three living men to vote in their place. The state rep won by three votes, he bragged. She was supposed to be impressed.

At another rally, she met a party regular who told her about his neighbor, who petitioned the tax board to lower her house taxes. She went before the board and made her appeal, stating that she was house rich but cash poor and would appreciate her taxes not being raised in the current re-evaluations. Needless to say, her house taxes were not raised. This pol was pleased that he could deliver a favor; you never knew when you would need one in return.

Maddie wasn't pleased to learn about such manipulations, but she rationalized that such acts were in the past and the current crop of candidates were of a different stripe. She prayed that that was true. A recent incident gave Maddie a new perspective on her campaign and American elections: she had been giving out her campaign literature in front of the neighborhood supermarket when a man started a conversation with her.

"I recently left Russia due to the increasing anti-Semitism there and we've only heard about American elections being free," he began in his slightly accented English, "but to see it in action isn't like a dream anymore, but a wonderful, thrilling event. I'm so thankful that I was able to get out of Russia and come to America, and then to see this . . ." he trailed off. Maddie had never given a thought to the wonder of free elections being held. She took them for granted. Now she had no choice but to cherish the process she was involved in. She related some of these stories to Jack, a man she was seeing. She mentioned the Russian man's story to him.

"That's very moving. He was lucky to get out and you were lucky to meet him. Only in America, eh?" They agreed that, from time to time, Americans needed to remember how blessed they are to hold elections, where results are routinely honored. Then Jack returned to the status of her campaign.

"So, it's going well?" he asked her that evening. They planned to see a movie at the Cable Car Theater. A small theater, it was an innovation in Providence: it had small sofas, more like loveseats, that could seat two, as well as armchairs instead of the standard seats in movie theaters.

"Oh, pretty good. The party is pleased that I'm walking my district because from their point of view it's one way of getting out the vote, getting people to know that there's a real live person running to represent them." She wrinkled her brow.

Jack laughed. "And . . .?"

"And I'm feeling pressure to debate the incumbent. Something I definitely don't want to do. She's a formidable debater, I'm sure.

Won't let go of an issue until she's chewed it to the bone. Friends of mine, whom she knows, have told me that she's called them to find out what I'm like and if there's any dirt she can use against me. They all say that they tell her I'm a wonderful person. I have no reason not to believe them, but her actions certainly up the stakes."

Jack cut to the chase. "So, don't debate her. The party wants a sacrificial lamb and you're it. You don't owe them anything beyond that."

Maddie breathed more freely after his response. "You're right. I'm doing everything else they want me to do: going to all the rallies, walking my district, which they really like. They even offered to have someone escort me for my evening walks of the district, just to be on the safe side. I pooh-poohed that. We live in a safe neighborhood."

"Who knows? I guess you're right, but you can never be too safe. Are you sure you don't want someone to walk with? I'd be happy to do it."

"I really feel very safe and I don't stay out late. Thanks for the offer. Besides it might just distract voters. I've never seen two people who were politicking come to my house."

"If you're sure. But still, it's true that this is a pretty safe area. It helps when you live in the same district as the mayor." Jack chuckled. "Just be sure to return before dark," he added.

Maddie liked walking alone in the early evening hours, able to reflect on how things were going, having no one with her to interrupt her meditations. Next week she would start walking the area of her district which she thought would be favorable to her opponent and not to her. She wasn't looking forward to it, but she had to bite that bullet. It was a matter of pride to her: to do what she had tacitly signed up for. She had no expectations of winning, but she wanted to at least make a good showing and have some clout in the party, to prove to herself that she could rise to a new challenge. If she were perfectly honest, she hoped for an upset and that she'd win, knowing full well that was a long shot.

It was a balmy night. Providence in summer was always lovely, many cool nights with light breezes. She and Jack walked to the movie house. That was one of the things she liked about Providence. You could walk to most places you needed to go. Or if you had to drive, it was a short trip to where you were going. People called a ten-minute drive a commute. Having lived in New York City, she could tell them what a real commute was.

LUISA

Rome, February 1944

Luisa had been pushed to her limit. She informed her contact that she needed a break from taking photos. To witness such situations was too demoralizing. She recognized that she was only *seeing* the suffering; Jews were *living* it. She had even heard of one who hid in a wood pile.

While reluctant to have her stop this aspect of the partisans' efforts, her contact Antonio, understood. Besides, he did have others who could take photos and he still needed *staffette* to deliver documents, weapons and messages. He needed to guard against complete burnout on Luisa's part.

A week later, Luisa awoke to clouds. She ate her breakfast of dry bread with no butter or jam to ease the dryness of the dense loaf and gulped a cup of chicory "coffee" to wash it down. By the time she set out on her delivery of a message, it was raining—not hard, but enough to make her want to crawl back into bed.

She pulled out her bike with the new alterations demanded by the Germans, set it on its stand, hid the message in her basket, and covered it with laundry. Then she covered that with lots of paper so that no one would think it strange that she was delivering laundry in the rain even though it was only a light drizzle.

She arrived at the drop-off area, but no one was there to receive the message. She looked around, but all she saw in the middle of the block was an old man limping along with an umbrella and his wife, Luisa presumed, lagging behind, getting wet, and grumbling something about his going out in the rain with his cold.

"*Signore*," Luisa said as she walked towards him, "may I help you? I have an extra umbrella that your wife might find helpful."

He brushed aside that question and asked, "Do you have anything else to give me?"

Luisa, troubled, looked at him. This wasn't the way it was supposed to go down. She was told to meet her contact alone at the corner, he coming from one direction and she from the other. Their arriving from opposite directions was accurate, but no one had said anything about a wife accompanying him. She temporized by fiddling with her umbrella.

"What else did you have in mind?" she asked.

"Whatever you can give at a corner, you can give here on this patch of sidewalk in the middle of the block."

She looked hard at him. Was he an informer? Why was another person with him?

"My friend Antonio says that anything can be given here as well as at the corner."

Luisa stared at him, suspicious. He had mentioned the name of her partisan contact. Could she trust him or had her contact fallen into enemy hands and the details of her drop divulged? Two men and a woman walked around them on the congested sidewalk. Luisa shifted her bike to make room for them. A few dry leaves, leftovers from the fall, lay sodden in the street.

"And why would he say that?" she demanded.

"Because my wife insisted on accompanying me and so, in trying to dissuade her—when she wants to do something, there's no saying no to her—it only made her more adamant to come along, even with this splash of rain. Women," he said in disgust.

"Your wife sounds like a strong-headed woman. What would Antonio say about that?"

"He'd say that my wife was concerned about me going out in the rain, and by insisting on coming with me, she hoped to dissuade me."

"And would he be right?" she asked.

"As right as rain." He chuckled. "But I'm as stubborn as she is and I came nonetheless." He leaned in and continued, "Look, all of us can't stand here in the rain, attracting attention. You must decide what you want to do so that we can all be on our way. I'm an old man, but you have a lot to lose by this dallying."

She stared at him long and hard. She recognized that she was in danger. His answers were too smooth. She decided not to take the chance. With that, she turned and, over her shoulder, said, "You're right. Perhaps we'll meet another time—at the corner."

The old man let out a deep sigh, turned to his wife, said something brusque to her, and started walking back from where they had come.

Luisa searched for clarity amidst the rain and the fog but found none. Only she could decide whether to trust this man or not. She knew enough about herself to realize that she tended to put the best interpretation onto a situation, but what was her alternative? To think everything was a trap? So far, she had negotiated well all the dilemmas that had arisen from her courier work.

"Stop."

The old man looked at Luisa. "Yes, what do you want?" he asked. Luisa dug into her basket, retrieved the message, and placed it in the palm of her hand. "It was very nice meeting you," she said, shook his hand and transferred the message into his palm.

"Ah, so," he answered, smiling. "You're a smart woman with good intuition." And with that he turned and left.

Luisa breathed a deep sigh of relief. Her instincts had been correct, thank God. She had taken a big chance in giving the message to the old man, but from the brusque words to his wife Luisa concluded that he was exasperated with her for tagging along and interfering with the drop. His actions rang true.

She had taken a chance but it turned out all right. At least, so far. He didn't stop her from leaving. The other couple who had been walking down the street hadn't returned to grab her. If he wasn't the contact, it would cause havoc for the partisan network and suffering for Antonio and for her.

Luisa started second-guessing herself. Perhaps his speaking to his wife that way was part of his act. She shook her head clear and squeezed her bike's handlebars. She'd only know what would follow from her action in the days to come. Please God, she prayed as she pedaled home, let there be no repercussions. Every aspect of what she was doing was dangerous.

ARTEMISIA

ROME, EARLY 1600S

Giorgio was an eager model. He came early and wandered around the studio until I was ready. He looked at my paintings with interest. This pleased me. Once a painting was sold, an artist never saw the reaction to her work of people other than the buyer.

"Artemisia," he said as I began his pose, "I liked the way you suggested the background on that painting. And how were you able to paint the lute to look so real? I almost thought that I'd begin to hear a song coming out of it."

"You've given me the highest compliment, Giorgio, by saying that you could almost hear a song coming from it. I worked very hard to make the strings look real and her fingers look as if they were strumming. Fingers are very hard to paint."

"You did that fine, Artemisia."

"And what's your opinion of the girl herself?"

"I think she hears her own song and is reacting to it. She likes what she hears herself playing and is thinking about the melody. It's a sad melody or, maybe not sad, but one that would make you start thinking about the beauty of music or—" He stopped. "Or who knows what. I'm just spinning tales, Artemisia." And with that he pressed his lips shut.

I was almost moved to tears that my painting of the woman with a lute could evoke so much feeling from an uneducated person. But that's what a painting should do . . . touch the emotions. A person didn't need to be educated or know what Galileo's latest theory was—though I have to admit: I loved talking to Galileo about his theories. One time when Galileo and I were discussing the heavens, I promised him that I would paint a star in one of my works to honor his studies. As for Giorgio's reactions to my work, it convinced me once again that a person just needed to look at a painting and feel the emotions that the artist stirred in him or her. The viewer finished the act of the artist's creation. The painting still needed work before it was finished to my satisfaction. The background needed more definition. And I had yet to decide what color would dominate the lute player's robes. I was torn between brown and gold. Brown would give her a solidity that I liked to show in my women, but how I loved the look of golden robes!

"Giorgio," I said, "I humbly thank you for your comments. They mean a lot to me. You understood my painting exactly." With that, I set to work, humming every now and then as I thought about what Giorgio had said.

He was pleased with what I had said about him. This time I placed him with his back facing me and his face turned towards me: I could see a smile forming on his profile while I delineated the muscles in his back. We both remained silent with our own thoughts. Peace reigned in the studio.

Peace wasn't the word I'd use to describe the atmosphere of my studio when Tassi arrived. Tension always seemed to swirl in the air when he entered. I couldn't figure out why. I did what he told me and he himself told me that I did it well. Was it that he had other things in mind besides instructing me?

I often caught him looking at me instead of the art chore he had set me. I had begun to take these lessons seriously. I wished he were as serious as I. Did he dismiss my work by not looking at it as intently as he looked at me, because I was a woman? Father had warned me that art—and everything else outside the home—was a man's world. I broached one aspect of that subject with Tassi.

"Do you think my art will gain the attention it deserves despite my being a woman?"

He was slow in answering and chose his words. "*Piccionina*," he began, using the diminutive for pigeon, "a woman artist will no doubt have difficulty in what is a man's world. But your talent will rise above such considerations."

I took comfort from some of what he said, but his referring to me as his little pigeon didn't sit well. After all, everyone knows that pigeon manure is used to fertilize plants. Perhaps I was being too negative. Could the pet name also suggest that I would fertilize the world of art with my paintings, made by me, a woman? My optimistic thoughts won out. I proceeded with our lesson for the day. Today he stressed the grinding of pigments. I proceeded. He leaned over me to see that I was grinding the vermilion finely enough. I was uncomfortable with feeling his body heavy against mine. I squirmed. His body relaxed and moved a bit away from mine. I continued to grind the pigments. His body again moved in against mine.

"Tuzia," I yelled. "Would you please hand me that other utensil for grinding? This one seems dull." Of course, that wasn't true, but at the moment it was all I could think of to get Tassi off me. Tuzia rose from her chair in the back of the studio and asked which one was she to bring me. I pointed to the instrument the third from the right. With heavy steps, she brought it to me. It had taken her long enough! As Tuzia ambled towards me, Tassi moved farther away from me. I breathed out and continued my pigment grinding. Enough was enough.

After the "lesson," I went to father.

"Father," I began, "I don't think I need any further lessons from Tassi. We seem to go over the same things forever. He had me back doing grinding."

"You'll continue with him as long as I say. We need to cultivate him to get commissions."

"If he hasn't named us yet as co-workers, he never will," I countered.

This meant nothing to Father and he continued to insist that I take lessons from Tassi, whether I was learning anything new or not. "That's not the point," he reiterated. "Think about the commissions,

Artemisia. We can use the work—and the money."

That was all that Father cared about. I didn't bother to tell him about Tassi's increasingly familiar behavior towards me. I was sure Father would just tell me I was imagining things, just as I imagined works of art into reality. How I wish I had insisted in the light of what happened later. But Father was even more insistent than I could have been: his work wasn't going well. He needed a new client and none was forthcoming. I went back to my studio, chastened.

Under Tassi, art was almost becoming a drudgery to me. But then Giorgio would enter my studio and I'd feel all the same excitement about my craft as I always did. Dear, sweet Giorgio always lifted my spirits.

"*Buon giorno*, Artemisia. How are you today?" His simplicity and innocence saved the day for me and pushed away bad thoughts about Tassi.

"I'm fine, Giorgio, and how are you? Have you done any more fishing?"

"I have. Next time I go I'll take you. You can look at the fish more closely once I've caught them."

I laughed. "You mean you always catch some when you go?"

"Oh yes. There are plenty in the water and they love my bait."

We made a date for me to go with him, along with Tuzia, of course. I wasn't particularly looking forward to it, but I wanted to humor Giorgio. He was so kind to me. Besides, I might actually learn something more about fish under his tutelage, but I couldn't see any use for it in my painting. And I'd be outside, taking a much needed break.

My drawings of fish did seem to improve a bit under Giorgio's tutelage. He showed me little things that I hadn't noticed. Not that I could think of a painting in which fish would be included. I just wanted to please him. He brightened my days with the generosity of his time posing for me. I put him into all sorts of contortions to highlight the shape of various muscles. He never complained or failed to hold a pose as long as I wanted him to.

Tassi showed up at one of our modeling sessions.

"Why are you wasting time doing this?" He almost screamed his question.

What difference did it make to him how I used my time when I didn't have a lesson with him? He stared at Giorgio but said nothing as he moved forward and tried to shove him off the platform he stood on. I had given Giorgio a sword to hold above his head to see how his muscles would react. I moved forward to stop Tassi. Giorgio resisted Tassi's force. They struggled while I ineffectually beat Tassi on the back. Though Giorgio was pushed off balance, he remained standing. Tassi lunged at Giorgio again. This time Giorgio had time to point the sword right at Tassi, who fell back and screamed again. Tuzia hadn't moved a muscle during this whole time but simply looked on at this scene from the back of the studio.

"What do you think you're doing?" Tassi bellowed, his clothes and hair in disarray.

"Artemisia and I are having a lesson. We'd appreciate your kindly not interrupting us again." Giorgio stood straight and to his full height with the sword pointing down at his side.

I was moved to silence, as was Tassi. Here was this boy—good for nothing as far as Tassi was concerned—who had more dignity than Tassi could fake. I felt triumphant.

"Please leave us," I said, forcing myself to speak as sweetly as possible. I didn't want to antagonize Tassi. His face dropped. He turned and slunk off, murmuring as he went, "She's having a *lesson* with *him*, humph. The most ridiculous thing I ever heard of." He squeezed out a laugh as he left.

Giorgio looked at me and burst into laughter. "What a fool," he said. "He acted as if he were the guardian of this studio."

"Or as if he were a god of this studio," I added and we both broke into laughter together until tears came to our eyes.

Father had heard the noise and came rushing in. "What's the problem?" he asked.

"No problem, Father. Just a little misunderstanding and a bit of confusion that followed. Everything's fine now, as you can see."

Father didn't pursue the matter any further. He saw that I was fine and Giorgio was back up on the platform, posing again. Where, I wondered, was Tuzia in all this? She was supposed to be looking out for me. Instead, she just sat at the back of the studio. What good was that?

MADDIE

Providence, August 1978

Maddie was excited as she got ready to walk her district. It had been arranged that she would be walking with United States Senator Claiborne Pell. A most decent man—although some Rhode Islanders called him Senator Stillborne Pell because of his torpid manner—he was one of those WASPs that Rhode Islanders voted for at the federal level.

He greeted her, if not warmly, in a gentlemanly manner. No surprise there, Maddie thought. They exchanged a few pleasantries and started on their walk of the district. She didn't think of the senator as a great campaigner, but his height and gracious manner as well as his legislative initiatives were sufficient for re-election. She remembered when she first heard of him, back in the '60s. It was his first run and one of his big initiatives was to legislate for grants to help students finance their higher education. That was enough to win him backers at Brown University, one of the largest employers in the state, and at every other university, college and community college in the area.

Rhode Island was in a state of flux, if not outright decline, away from manufacturing to service employment. Maddie had recently gone to a union rally featuring an old-time union supporter. The woman brought down the house when she said that the textile industry would rise again in Rhode Island; she was stuck in the 1940s. All the textile mills had gone south then, where cheaper labor was available. Rhode Islanders could only hope that their jewelry businesses, one of the few major manufacturing businesses still in Rhode Island, wouldn't leave.

Senator Pell had targeted a good segment of the population when he focused on education. His initiative had passed in what came to be called the Pell Grants. Unfortunately, his other initiative in education, monies to support vocational training, was less popular and had yet to gain ground. But he still talked about it as he and Maddie made their way from house to house, but mainly he didn't talk about his policies. Rather he greeted voters with a handshake, asked how they were, and made some general comments.

At one house—Maddie couldn't remember how it came about—he started talking in Italian. Maddie joined in, to the senator's delight, speaking what she called her pigeon Italian.

They moved on to the area that Maddie thought would favor her opponent. She was glad to have the senator along for this section. She had dreaded calling on these houses. The senator rang the bell of the first house in the area. As they moved on to other houses in the district, Maddie was surprised to find that this section of her district was different from what she had anticipated. She was completely wrong about its sympathies. She had a lot to learn about her district, but she *was* learning. After walking along another block, the senator said goodbye and climbed into his limousine. Maddie would have to continue by herself. She knew now that she could do this.

Maddie had been invited to meet with the party's state chairman at an event. She was told to meet him at a small auditorium where he was giving a presentation. He was tall, charismatic even with his slicked back hair, good looks and modulated speaking voice. None of that bellowing, so common among politicians, came from him. After his talk she introduced herself, telling him the district she was running in.

"Yes, I hear you're doing a good job, walking that district. That's good. That's important."

"I just wish that people would talk about something other than potholes."

He laughed. "They're always a problem."

"The potholes or the people?"

He laughed again. "So other than that, how's it going?"

"I think pretty well. I'd like to run a newspaper ad to get the word out to reinforce my visits, to make it look like I'm a real contender, and do some more mailings, but I don't have the money for that." Maddie eyed the chairman, all the time knowing what she was doing, and he knowing what she was doing as well. He studied her until Maddie started to feel uncomfortable, but she didn't shift her eyes from his face.

"OK. I'll see what I can do about freeing up some money for that. Tell me what else you've been doing."

Maddie mentioned her outreach to different groups in her district. She gave as examples talks she had given to some educators and other groups, which had been well received. She told him that she had blanketed the area with her stickers. During one such foray with her campaign manager (she smiled in embarrassment as she thought about it) they were stopped by a cop from continuing to paste her signs on lamp posts.

"Those things happen. But you made the effort and were mostly successful. I've seen your bumper stickers on a number of cars too. That's good." He stood to leave. Maddie shook his hand and was on her way home, one more task accomplished. She thought she'd get the money.

Maddie was making the rounds again of political rallies. She was with Deedee, a widow she had met at a fundraising function. Deedee was a generous donor to the party and was appreciated by one and all.

She was tall and slim with a face that would haunt you, and not for the better. But oh, what legs! Long and gorgeous. What Maddie liked about her, really enjoyed, was that Dee was upbeat, always ready to laugh. A lot of fun to be with.

Tonight, she wore a black, mid-calf, lacy dress. She admitted to Maddie that it was actually a nightgown which she had teamed up with a full slip underneath. She looked great. That was typical Deedee.

Maddie was talking to some of her constituents when Dee came over. "Come over here," she said and then whispered, "You don't want to talk to them: they're not people."

Maddie immediately understood what Dee was saying: don't waste your time on them. Talk to the politicians. She had to laugh and this became a common line between the two of them, Maddie teasing Dee about it and Dee laughing as heartily as Maddie. That was another thing she liked about Dee. She could laugh at herself.

In her youth, Dee told Maddie, she had been a dancer, one of those background dancers who were ubiquitous in shows. She was perfectly content to stay in the background. She didn't want to be the lead dancer—too much pressure. What she hoped was that she'd meet someone to marry. And she did. One of the producers was a hometown boy who had made good and stayed in New York City. Now widowed for a number of years, Dee returned to her hometown of Providence and harbored the same hope: to marry someone, this time a politician. Or if not that, at least to find a bedmate.

LUISA

Rome, March 1944

Luisa woke with a start. She looked around to get her bearings. She lay in her own bed with its coverlet askew. She was shivering. Shivering from fear. She had dreamt that she was floating through the air in a parachute, enjoying the ride, looking at the sites below: the Colosseum, the Forum, both bathed in sunlight when suddenly the sky turned black. She twisted this way and that, squirmed in her parachute. It was choking her. She tried to untangle herself, but it only got tighter. She kept falling closer to earth but couldn't straighten out the lines of the chute. She pulled on the line to release the parachute, to no avail. She kept falling faster and faster. The night sky was studded with stars. She thought how beautiful the sky was. She wondered why she was now focused on the sky instead of getting the chute to open. She forced herself to pull on the line again. Again, to no avail. She started to scream as she hurtled through the air, faster and faster, rushing down to the *Curia Giulia*, where the Roman senators met in the Forum. It was then that she woke up, her sheets twisted around her.

Her shivering had stopped but she was breathing fitfully, gasping for air. She wiped her forehead; perspiration had formed despite her feeling cold. She pushed off the covers, got up, stumbled to the kitchen and poured herself a glass of water from the pitcher she had filled. She scrutinized the four walls to convince herself that she was still in the apartment she shared with her mother. Reassured, she tiptoed back to bed.

It didn't take a genius to interpret her dream, she thought. Her nerves were shot working for the partisans. She had had her share of close calls, the latest being the drop with the old man whose wife had followed him. So far there had been no repercussions. This should have calmed her but it didn't. She was wound tight.

She got up from bed again and decided to read something soothing. She scrutinized the books on her shelves and dismissed them all. Finally, she took out the Bible, a book she rarely read, and opened to the Psalms. She shuffled through a few pages. "The Lord is my shepherd," she read. "I shall not want. He maketh me to lie down in green pastures." Her breathing began to slow and regulate itself. She had to get hold of herself or her lack of ease would cause her to make an inadvertent error on her next drop.

The Bible passage comforted her after she repeated it at least half a dozen times. She started to get dressed. She had a meeting this morning with Antonio, her partisan contact. She prepared breakfast quickly; she was running late and rushed out of the house with her half piece of toast in hand. She arrived at their meeting place, a spot that was all rubble and obscured by mist. She sat down on a large rock amidst the squalor. Antonio was already there. He made no greeting, nor, as usual, did he use her name.

"We need you to take a photo of a Jew in hiding. It needs to be done this morning. I know you prefer not to do this sort of job, but this one's important. Don't let me down. I can't find anyone else to do it."

Lucia struggled with herself. Not only did she not want to let the partisans down, she didn't want to let herself down, and yet . . . She was silent for a full minute.

"Well?" prompted Antonio.

"Only if you promise me this will be the last time. You know I'm dedicated to the Resistance and if you can't get anyone else, I'll do it. But I'm asking you to send someone else. There must be someone else who can do it."

"But there isn't. Everyone's busy on some other important matters that have come up. As to this being the last time I ask you, I need to weigh the pros and cons." He fidgeted with his keys. "You know I can't promise that. I can only assure you that this will be one of the last times that we call upon you to do this. This is an important person, whom we need to get out of the country fast."

Luisa knew better than to ask who this person was. She silently prayed, "The Lord is my shepherd. I shall not want. He maketh me to lie in green pastures." The ride to the countryside will do me good, she thought. Rome is making me claustrophobic and a change of scene in open countryside will restore me to some kind of equilibrium.

She told Antonio she would do it. She was glad for the strength she was able to call up. She was to return to the same house where she had gone to take photos of the three-generational family. She concluded that meant that they must have gotten out of Italy, or at least moved on to something better. This thought energized her. It reassured her that her work had value. She thought about all that those two young children, like so many others, were experiencing. No one should have to go through that. She hurried home to get her camera and bike. She wished she could pack a picnic lunch of bread and cheese and eat in the countryside, but she knew that was a long-gone wish. It was inhumane for the Germans to keep all the food for themselves. Food that in ordinary times was actually precious to Italians: bread, for those who were religious, connected to the sacrament of communion. Its deprivation was unjust.

The ride was already doing her good. Her breathing was normal. She concentrated on the beauty of God's creation as she repeated the psalm that comforted her. The words, with their simple beauty and rhythm, soothed her. The sun had broken through the mist and warmed the crisp air of the countryside. It infused her with hope— hope that the evil that stalked Europe would be replaced by a more stable peaceful era of civility and humane conduct. She seemed to arrive at the farmhouse in no time at all.

Luisa hid her bike in the barn. Then she knocked on the door as usual. "I was hoping you had some eggs I could buy. My mother wants to make a *frittata*." They followed the same script as before and she entered the farmhouse. She greeted its residents and then climbed up the twisted staircase to the attic and entered the room. An older man sat silently in a straight-backed chair. Though his face was gaunt, it was a kind face, one that had seen trouble. Is he a rabbi, Luisa wondered, or the leader of the network to keep the Jews informed as to what was happening? She whispered a greeting. He made no acknowledgment except to nod his head slightly. Luisa wanted to reassure this gentleman that he'd be safe here, but his silence inhibited her. How could she, who was so young, dare to give comfort to a man who had probably seen much too much sorrow already?

She began to set up her camera for the photo. Her thoughts were interrupted by sounds from downstairs. Someone had banged on the front door. Luisa froze as did the man. She strained to hear. She heard the door open, some words spoken in a harsh, commanding voice. The next thing she heard was a German, questioning the husband and wife. Luisa thought they responded by denying any knowledge of people hiding in the area, neither Jews, partisans, escaped prisoners of war, nor former Italian soldiers. Then she heard footsteps on the stairs. The soldiers, accompanying their German superior, were going up to the second floor, where the bedrooms were. She heard doors opening, objects being swept aside, chaos occurring as items were smashed to the floor. Her heart was racing. She was sure that the whole house could hear it beating. Luisa peered at the man. He remained as unruffled as before, his face giving nothing away.

She heard the Germans tramping down the hall, back towards the stairs, creaking at each footfall. The soldiers' footsteps were slowing down as each step caused greater groaning and screaming of the stairs. To Luisa, the noise sounded deafening. She plastered her trembling hands over her ears. When the men reached the bend in the stairway leading to the attic, Luisa was wild-eyed. She couldn't think; she didn't dare breathe. And still the gentleman remained calm while her heart plummeted to her rib cage.

Just as the Germans were about to proceed to the part of the stairs that turned back on itself, she heard the leader of the group issue a command and what sounded like feet sliding and turning on the stair. And then she heard the footfalls moving farther away. The Germans were climbing back down the stairs. She didn't trust her ears. Frozen in place, she listened to the marching feet stomping across the first floor. She heard the front door open, boots marching through, and then the door slammed shut. The Germans were gone. She couldn't believe it. Nor could she move. What if their leaving was just a ruse to flush out whoever was in hiding and then they would return to arrest them? She waited for what seemed like an eternity, not moving a muscle. The gentleman did the same, his eyes burning into her.

Again, Luisa heard footsteps on the stair. Her head snapped up. This time she recognized the light footfalls of the couple who owned the house.

"As you were," the husband said. "The soldiers have left. Thank God the rain started again and scared those brave—" here he laughed, "—soldiers, who were too lazy to deal with the rickety stairs and its bend to the attic. And, of course, they didn't want to get their beautiful boots wet once the rain fell in earnest."

Luisa gave a shrill cackle. Her nerves were shot. She put her head in her hands and cried unashamedly. When she composed herself, she proceeded to take the gentleman's photo and then staggered down the stairs, feeling as if her footsteps were loud enough for the whole countryside to hear. On the advice of the couple, Luisa waited until the soldiers would have been far away from the farmhouse. She sat by the small fire, just big enough to take the chill off her bones. Once again, she left with two eggs in her pocket in case a German stopped to question her about what she was doing in the countryside. She was just looking for a little justice, looking for food.

ARTEMISIA

Rome, early 1600s

"What's my lesson today to be?" Giorgio and I were standing outside my studio. After our last session, he said he would teach me about flowers. I didn't care a fig about flowers, but I did enjoy being in nature and eagerly accepted whatever he proposed. I needed a break from my usual routine.

I felt free when I was with him. He had no expectations of me. He demanded nothing. I left behind the problems associated with obtaining a commission, the reason my father wanted me to work with Tassi. I left the problems of working out the placement of figures in my latest painting to another time. I had confidence that everything would work out while I was on my jaunt with Giorgio.

It was a lovely day, not a cloud in the sky and the sun shone brightly but not hot. The birds were warbling and I embraced it all. Giorgio was quiet, which suited me fine. Enough people talked to me, always giving directions. If it wasn't my father, it was Tassi. If it wasn't Tassi, it was Tuzia complaining about something that I had no control over.

We strolled side by side. Tuzia, following behind, tut-tutted at my high spirits. Giorgio was taking me to one of his favorite gardens, a fairly small one with a profusion of blooms on the outskirts of the city. There were roses and day lilies, coreopsis and hydrangeas and a dozen other flowers. Giorgio showed me the stamens of each along with the other parts of the flowers. It was so good to be away from Father and Tassi. We wandered through winding paths, breathing in the lovely fragrances, alone in our private world.

Song birds twittered among the trees. Father thought of song birds as potential food. They were considered a delicacy. I could never bring myself to eat one. I found the thought of killing such a creature, who gave us nothing but joy, repulsive. They were pure joy, as far as I was concerned.

"Giorgio," I said, leaning towards him, "thank you so much for taking me here. It's just the respite I needed."

"What does respite mean?"

"The rest and peace I find here in this beautiful garden with you."

He beamed. We ambled along for a while and then he stopped and turned towards me. "Artemisia..."

He stood there motionless and just gazed into my eyes and I returned his gaze. We were two young people feeling the pull of the attraction we each had for the other. Giorgio's attraction was different from mine. As a young man, he didn't have to worry about the same things that I, as a young woman, had to think about. I knew how men could ruin young women by forcing sex on them and then saying it was consensual. Hadn't my mother told me stories in the Bible about such situations? Tuzia's constant presence was my safeguard against any such thing happening to me.

I was very appreciative of the comfort Giorgio gave me but it went no farther than that. We were from two different worlds and I was well aware of that. It was Father who would decide who and when I would marry. It wasn't my decision to make. I had to make sure that I didn't compromise myself in any way before marriage.

Giorgio reached for my hand. I didn't protest. That too was comforting. I took his other hand and started swinging our arms side to side. He stood before me content and then, letting go of one hand, he twirled me around. We were both drunk with the sheer gladness we gave each other. It was exhilarating. I was very fond of him. Giorgio was such a sweet boy.

On our way back to the studio, we ran into Tassi, who put an end to a perfect day.

"Good day," he said.

We both responded in kind.

"Been out for a walk on this beautiful day?"

"Yes, Giorgio was pointing out some flowers he was fond of and which I might find useful in my painting."

"Better to use your time painting than traipsing around Rome, looking at flowers."

"I can decide what's best for me, thank you, *maestro*." Though I was gritting my teeth, I spoke as sweetly as I could so as not to alienate him.

With that, Tassi grabbed my arm and pushed me in the direction of the studio. "You don't know what's best for you, you little fool," he said.

Giorgio stepped forward and pushed down on Tassi's arm, releasing his hold on me. Tassi was enraged. "Don't you ever touch me again," he yelled at Giorgio.

"And don't you ever touch Artemisia again," he yelled back.

With that, Tassi lunged at Giorgio. "Who do you think you are, talking to me like that?" He grabbed Giorgio by his collar and began shaking him.

"Stop," I yelled. "Stop, stop."

But he didn't stop. Tassi and Giorgio tussled some more. A small crowd was forming around them. I feared what Father would say if he learned of this. I was supposed to stay on Tassi's good side for the sake of getting him to recommend Father and me for a commission to help him paint.

I spotted one of the neighborhood boys. "Please, Franco," I said, "try to stop them. I don't want either of them to get hurt." Franco took one of his friends with him as he approached Tassi and Giorgio. They separated them and held their arms so that they couldn't hurt each other any further. I rushed over to Giorgio. "Please Giorgio, let's go."

Then I turned to Tassi and said, "I hope you'll let bygones be bygones and just think of this as a terrible misunderstanding. You must realize that I can't work twenty-four hours a day, just as you can't. You were out walking on this beautiful day just as I was. Please, let us be friends again." Tassi gave me a curt nod, glared at Giorgio, turned and walked away. All this time, Tuzia had stayed out of the fray and just looked on, bored by all the turmoil. I prayed she wouldn't tell Father about this incident or that he wouldn't hear of it from someone else.

No sooner had I sat down to supper with Father than he confronted me. As best as I could, I explained to him that it was all a misunderstanding, but Father would have none of it. He forbade me to see Giorgio again. I pleaded with him, explaining how much I was learning about male musculature from Giorgio's posing for me. Father was loath to hear anything from me.

"What if I only saw Giorgio in the studio? I wouldn't go on any outings with him, I promise."

"No," was Father's curt reply.

"My paintings will be more valuable the more accurate I am in depicting the male body. Please think about that and reconsider."

"I'll think about it and get back to you."

I thought this argument would be persuasive with Father. He hoped to benefit from my painting. The better I painted, the better for him. Everything he had ever done was to help me be a great painter so that my artworks would fetch large amounts of money. My growth as an artist really didn't interest him. He hadn't engaged Tassi as my mentor for my sake. Money was his concern.

MADDIE

PROVIDENCE, AUGUST 1978

Maddie had already covered more than half her district. The higher-ups were pleased, even if she didn't see a groundswell for her candidacy. She attended all the rallies and meetings that various groups held. Her friends held coffees for her. Today she was to go to an event held by a college president in Rhode Island. It was a musicale for some donors that the college was "cultivating," in the lingo of fundraising. As a Providence resident running for political office in the state, Maddie has been invited. You never knew when the college might need a favor.

The house of the college president was one of understated elegance. The musicale took place in a large comfortable room, overlooking a garden. The president and his wife greeted every guest as each passed along a receiving line. Maddie commented to the president's wife on their garden and later on continued that topic of conversation. Maddie mentioned that she had a quince tree, which interested the wife because she had a recipe for quince and she hadn't been able to find any at the food stores. Maddie promised to bring her some when they were fully ripe.

The musicale was lovely. The musicians played some seventeenth-century Italian music, not exactly anything on the pop charts. The potential donors seemed to enjoy it well enough, and then they adjourned to the garden for hors d'oeuvres and liquid refreshment. Maddie made the rounds, being sure to speak to as many people as possible. Some knew her name from her campaigning; others didn't have a clue.

She spoke to one person, who agreed with her support for vocational education. "I'm all for vocational education," a Mr. Durand said. "Not everyone has to go to college."

Maddie chimed in. "Nor does everyone *want* to go to college. Plus, the expense for a lot of people is prohibitive."

"Exactly," Mr. Durand said. "And for what? To be in debt and not prepared for any job. Some people, who just aren't interested in college, would be interested in a hands-on job. No shame in that."

"I agree. And I hope that I'll be able to convince some legislators to support funds for voc-ed." That was an easy one, Maddie thought, when someone already agrees with you about an issue. The hard ones are those who are diametrically opposed to your viewpoint. Maddie had spoken to someone of that persuasion: a Mrs. Paulson, who was against bilingual education.

"Not even one course should be taught in a language other than English." The woman was short and gaunt with a beehive hairdo from the 1960s. "How will they ever learn to speak English?"

"The benefit," Maddie said, "is that students won't miss important information in science and math, which could prevent them from going on to higher education."

"That's a point, but they won't succeed in getting to college if they can't speak English."

"But bilingual education is not forever. It's only a stopgap method for a year or two until the student is proficient in English, learned from their other classes and from their peers. Kids learn a lot of English from their peers. They want to be one of the group and that's one of their motivations to learn English."

"But bilingual education never seems to stop. Students go on and on with it."

And so went the discussion round and round. Maddie finally excused herself. A barrel-chested man, powerfully built, introduced himself. Maddie knew of him; he was a former college basketball star, who never left Rhode Island. What he liked best was schmoozing with the alums. Older men seemed to enjoy hearing about Don's glory days and listening to his sophomoric jokes. Maddie and he talked awhile about their times at college, reminisced about the graduation dance, and chit-chatted about the current generation of students.

It was getting dark and Maddie wanted to be home early. She had a long day of campaigning ahead of her tomorrow. She thanked her hosts for a lovely evening and headed towards the door. Don followed. No sooner were they out the door than Don's hands were all over her and under her dress. Maddie was taken aback but kept her cool. She quickly removed his hands and straightened her clothes.

"Slow down, cowboy. That's not my thing." Briefly, she wondered if she had flirted with him or given him an idea that she was open to his advances. But she definitely thought not. She wasn't at all attracted to him. She thought of him as an overgrown boy, who was reliving a presumed wild youth; someone who was still living his days as a basketball hero.

He persisted. "Why don't you come over to my place on Benevolent Street—not far from the Lightning House? You know where that is in Providence, don't you?"

Maddie smirked at the name of the street, so far from his intentions. "I can't, thank you. I have a busy day tomorrow." No point in being impolite and making an enemy. Didn't the state chairman tell her, "You never know when you'll need a friend"? That was the coin of the political realm—never make an enemy—and she was now in that world. She didn't want to make a big deal about this incident, but inwardly she was seething. She was a mature woman and could handle it, but what about some of the young women who were propositioned in this manner and the man not held accountable or even thought to be inappropriate in his actions? Just boys being boys, they'd protest. Honestly, she thought. And with that she walked to her car. On her way home, she passed by the Lightning House, with its incredibly steep gable because, before lightning rods, the later renovators of the 1781 house thought such a shape would ward off lightning. If only it could ward off more than that, Maddie thought.

Maddie got ready for bed. She couldn't stop thinking about the "fastest hands in the West." She had never experienced anything like that: his lightning speed, his total lack of interest in her feelings or in her as a human being. She was just a piece of meat. She realized how totally sheltered she was, and thanked God for that, but she kept thinking about those young girls.

A few days later, Maddie looked forward to Jack coming over. She needed to unload. Despite her visibility, she knew she wasn't doing well in her campaign. Nothing had caught fire. As she observed other campaigns, she saw that the candidates curried favor with a number of different segments of the population. Senator Pell reached out to people whose children wanted to attend college, but needed help financially. He also reached out to students who didn't want to go to college, but who needed to train for good-paying jobs. Therefore, he supported vocational education.

Providence, and Rhode Island generally, was foundering. The textile mills, which had been a big base of manufacturing in the state, had left for the cheaper wages offered in the South, never to return. The jewelry industry, which was made up of big manufacturers like Monet, as well as mom and pop shops, was failing and nothing had come along to take its place.

She needed to think of things that her constituents wanted. But what did they want? Potholes fixed! The East Side, which was Maddie's district, was a well-off section of the city. What would the people there want? She didn't know. Good schools probably, but what could she offer in that regard? Smaller classes, she supposed, but that was a city issue, not a state one—though she could look at the formula by which schools received money from the state. Perhaps the formula wasn't fair to all Providence schools, such as the ones in the disadvantaged areas. Yes, she would definitely look into that.

Some of Providence's artistic community resided around Wickenden Street on the outskirts of the Portuguese neighborhood in Fox Point. What would they want? Cheaper rents for their apartments and tiny galleries and shops. She didn't think that was a state issue.

Her front doorbell rang. Maddie went to the door to let Jack in. She was loath to tell him about what happened with Don. She was afraid of his reaction, but she could talk with him about issues to develop. A sounding board always helped.

As she opened the door, she was thankful to see Jack's kind face. Jack was tall, slim, good looking in a man's man kind of way. He wore glasses and had a small indentation on his forehead from a hockey injury years ago. Jack was an excellent athlete. He had won state tournaments. He was so humble that he had never told her the details. As a matter of fact, he hadn't brought it up at all. A mutual friend had filled her in. He was generous with his time. Maddie was a terrible athlete, but he took the time to play tennis with her and give her pointers in a low-key, non-judgmental way. She liked that aspect of him.

"Hi Jack. Good to see you."

"You look tired."

"Maybe not so much tired as discouraged."

"About what?"

"I haven't come across an issue that really grabs people."

"Give yourself time. You're new at this and something will eventually turn up as you continue meeting your constituents."

"I hope you're right."

"Maybe you need a break from it all. Sometimes when you don't think about a subject, the answer pops up."

"That's true."

"Haven't you ever had that experience?" He pulled her close.

"You're right. I have." She liked the feeling of being close to him. She sank into his body. They went upstairs.

When they came down, Maddie started supper. She was making spaghetti *carbonara*. It was her favorite comfort food. She put on the water for the spaghetti and got out the bacon, cheese and eggs. It was a fail-safe recipe. Jack scrambled the two eggs and added lots of parmesan cheese while Maddie cooked the bacon. Then she crumbled the cooked bacon, drained the pasta, and put it all together with a good grind of black pepper. They sat at the kitchen table to eat.

"Mm-m," Jack said as he took a second helping.

"It *is* good, isn't it?" Maddie said.

"Feel better about things?"

"Absolutely."

They cleared the dishes and put them into the dishwasher. Jack washed the pots.

"If you don't mind, I'd like to read the *Providence Journal*. I didn't have a minute to myself today to do that."

"Go ahead. I'll fix that window problem you've been having in the attic."

"Thanks so much, Jack. You're a sweetheart."

He started up the stairs as Maddie grabbed the newspaper and went into the living room to read it. She sank into her favorite armchair and started at page one.

When Jack returned, he found Maddie staring into space, deep in thought. She looked at Jack.

"I think I may have found an issue. I was just reading that the feds have upped the amount of money that can be left to people tax-free."

"You mean the inheritance tax?"

"Yeah, or as some call it, the death tax. And yet Rhode Island still has the lower figure that's tax-free. What if I proposed that Rhode Island maintain parity with the feds? This is a well-off district and a lot of the people in it might go for raising the amount of money you can leave to your heirs without paying any taxes. What do you think?"

"I think you're on to something. It's a great beginning."

Maddie felt that it *was* a good issue. She smiled as she thought about her late father, Dan. He had been the child of poor Italian immigrants who began to do well financially once he learned about

Wall Street and investing.

His older brother had been secretary to a broker and had taught Dan all about investing. Poor Mike, though, went through three fortunes and finally went broke in 1929, at the beginning of the Great Depression. He had been a high liver, traveling to Europe with his girlfriend, bringing back expensive gifts—a clock that chimed on the hour and the half hour, hand embroidered linens, leather goods—but, like so many high rollers at the time, he bought stock on margin.

When the Depression hit, he couldn't pay off what he owed on his margin buying. Maddie's father was a more conservative buyer; he never bought what he didn't have the money for. He wasn't interested in getting rich quick. He just wanted to ensure that any money he saved from his printing business grew so that he'd have something to leave to his future heirs—such a wild dream for a child who grew up with nothing and was left nothing except an optimistic personality and a belief in America.

Dan sold some of his stock to help his brother. He didn't want Mike to do something crazy. After all, men who had lost fortunes were jumping out of windows.

The two brothers studied Dan's portfolio. They decided to sell either his stock in General Motors or the Reo Motorcar Company. They chose to keep the Reo stock, where Maddie's mother had worked as a secretary before her marriage. In later years, Dan could laugh about missing out on becoming a millionaire by selling the GM stock. The decision had been based on nostalgia rather than being a reasoned one. Reo eventually folded as the Big Three car companies became dominant. Such was life in the stock market.

But as Dan aged, he groused more and more about what he called the death tax. "From rags to riches to rags in three generations," he'd moan. Maddie shook her head from side to side as she remembered her father's rant. He minded paying high taxes and she figured her Rhode Island constituents, too, would mind paying higher rates than the federal government required. She laughed out loud as she thought about how pleased her father would have been to make lowering Rhode Island's estate tax part of her platform.

Just then the phone rang. Maddie got up to answer it. "Hello?"

"This is Officer O'Connor. We have a situation: a guy on a roof who's threatening to jump off if you don't come. He's totally out of control, a crazy man."

"Wha—? What are you talking about?"

"Like I said, a guy wants to talk to you or he'll jump off a roof if you don't come."

"What do you mean? 'If I don't come'?"

"He's saying something about his fiancée being raped and is a basket case and he wants you, as a woman, if you're elected, to do something specifically for women who've been raped."

"Does he know that I'm lagging in the polls? Anyway, I can't promise that at this point, though I'm certainly sympathetic to the situation of such women."

"So, lady, will you come to talk to him?" Maddie was quiet for a moment, thinking about the implications of her agreeing to go. Finally, she said, "Of course, if you think I can be helpful."

"We've tried everything else for the last couple of hours. I'll pick you up in ten minutes tops."

She filled Jack in on the call. He was concerned for her safety.

"Does he have a weapon?"

"The officer didn't say. What he said was that the guy was threatening to jump off the roof of a building."

"I'll come with you. If I feel you're in danger, I'll drag you out of there. OK?"

"OK."

The officer arrived in seven minutes flat. They wound through streets, deserted at this hour, dark bleak buildings standing guard over the gloom. They passed three-decker houses, which seemed eerie without lights. The leaves of trees hung ghostly as the breeze rustled them. The policeman took her and Jack to the building, a four-story brick. Police cars surrounded the building and a reporter, along with a photographer, were there from the *Providence Journal*, the state's main newspaper.

"I want to talk to her privately," the man yelled down when he saw her arrive. "Send her up here right now or I jump." He started to put a leg over a wall around the perimeter of the roof.

"Wait a minute. Let me see what she says, but no way is she going up there alone," the officer answered. The man stiffened his leg over the wall and leaned his upper body forward.

"Then I'm jumping."

"OK, OK. Calm down. I didn't say she wasn't coming up. I'm just saying that we have to be sure you won't hurt her, buddy. Hold on, for god's sake and let me see what we can do."

Jack and Maddie conferred with the officer, all the while monitoring the man's movements. Against the head policeman's advice, but with his reluctant consent given the stalemate, he decided that Jack would go with her and pat down the guy to be sure he had no weapons. With that decided, Maddie addressed the jumper.

"If you want me to come up, you need to trust me and calm down a little. First, I want you to move away from the edge of the wall. Once you do that, I'll come up as you want, but my boyfriend's coming up with me. Those are my terms." The man froze his leg midway over the wall. He considered her proposition. Maddie went on to explain that Jack would then stay on the roof a slight distance away so that Maddie and the man would have privacy.

"Just no tricks," he yelled, losing control again. "How do I know he's not a cop? How do I know I can trust you?"

"You don't," Maddie yelled up. "But you saw him come with me, didn't you? As for trusting me, you asked me to come here. I didn't just show up. How do I know I should trust you, that you won't hurt me, huh? You need to calm down and trust me. OK? Take three deep breaths, move away from the wall and then let me know your answer."

The man, whose name they learned was Pete, considered this, shuffled four steps back from the wall, and then agreed to Maddie's terms after repeating that he wanted privacy.

Maddie and Jack trudged up the four flights of stairs of the deserted building, their heels echoing in the silence, and pushed open the door to the roof. It was murky. They searched the shadows for Pete. Maddie felt relieved that the roof had a four-foot wall at its perimeter. She was afraid of heights. They saw a movement on the far end of the roof.

"Pete?" asked Jack.

"Yeah."

"I'm coming over to check you out for weapons."

"No tricks, OK? I don't want any tricks. You understand? Or I jump in a minute. You got that, buddy?" He sneered as he said that last word, *buddy*.

Jack ignored the sarcasm and walked straight to the man while Maddie stood by the doorway. "Hi, buddy. I'm going to pat you down as we agreed. OK? Just relax. This won't take me long."

"Yeah, yeah. I coulda told you I didn't have any weapons. Isn't that what I said?"

Pete complied, though his body twitched every now and then. Jack attempted to relieve the man's anxiety by speaking in whispers, explaining what he was doing at each stage as he patted Pete down. Jack was slow and thorough, starting at his shoulders and working his way down Pete's body. Pete began to quiet down. His breathing became more regular. "OK. Maddie's going to walk over to you and I'm going to stand nearby, but far enough away that I can't hear you. OK?" The man nodded.

"But no tricks and no fast movements."

Though Pete was obsessed with his own safety, his speech was less anxious. Maddie was more relaxed than she thought she'd be. She walked over to him and said hello. "I'm Maddie. I heard you wanted to talk to me. My first question is, why me?"

Pete wiped the perspiration from his forehead against his sleeve and sighed. "I want you to win. I think you have a chance. I heard you speak at one of the party's rallies. This situation with me will get you some publicity." His staccato speech belied his calm, but he made an effort to stay rational and coherent. "The incumbent can't get what I want through the state senate. She's in the wrong party. Her opposition never lets her legislative initiatives pass. That's why I need you to win."

Maddie was confused. She wasn't sure what he was referring to. Nonetheless, to keep him calm and talking, she spoke conciliatory words in her most soothing voice, "I see. For such an extreme action that you've taken, you've thought this through very carefully, very rationally."

"Yeah, what I want is a promise that, if you're elected, you'll find funding for a house where women who've been raped can go for counseling and with the possibility of staying overnight right after. My fiancée needs help. She was raped a couple of weeks ago and the only thing that's happened is that she's been examined by a doctor, who confirms that she's been raped.

"But she's a basket case. What she needs is some sympathetic woman to talk to. To give her some help in living through this crime against her." He started talking faster and faster. "She can't work. She can't sleep. She just cries a lot. It's tearing me apart to see her suffering like this. Can you help her?" His words started to run into each other. "Do you know how I feel, knowing that some dumb-ass guy violated her like that?" Pete was close to weeping. He wiped his nose with the back of his hand and leaned against the wall.

"I don't know, but I can imagine how hard it is for you too. I could help her find a therapist with expertise in cases such as this to help her get past this terrible crime."

"That would be a good first step," he said. "She won't let me touch her. Not even hold her hand. Do you know what that's like, not being able to touch the person you love, not even her hand? She says she doesn't want to get married. Now she doesn't want to have kids. No kids. We're both from big families. We were looking forward to raising a brood of our own. We're into family, you know? This thing has destroyed everything we were looking forward to—everything . . . our future. I feel like I'm floating, floating away. Most of the time, she won't even talk to me. All she says is, 'It's all been said before.' When I ask her what's been said before, she just repeats that. 'It's all been said before' and then she nods her head and stares at me and nods her head some more."

"I'm so very, very sorry to hear all that you're both going through. It's the toughest thing you'll have to face for a long time. I can see you've thought carefully about this and what a woman in that situation would need. But I can't make such a promise. I don't know if I'll even be elected. You're assuming a lot. What if I didn't find any funding after having promised you? All I can do is promise that I'd try very hard to find funding for such an undertaking. *If* I'm elected," she repeated. "It's certainly worthwhile and there's no doubt in my mind that it's needed. No doubt whatsoever."

"You've gotta understand. Nothing I say matters to her now. Our lives, my life with the only woman I've ever loved, is going down the drain. I've known her since sixth grade. She was such a feisty little kid, even with her little curls, shaking on her head. I'm losing all we've worked towards. My heart doesn't beat anymore." Pete caught his breath. Maddie was silent, trying to take in all that he had said.

Pete remained quiet too. Then he said, "I understand." He took another deep breath or two. He knew that he didn't have much bargaining power. He'd already used his ace and he had no intention of jumping off the roof. He had said that to get Maddie there. He'd accomplished that. He'd have to take his chances with her.

Finally, he said, "Your promise is good enough for me. I never wanted to cause all this upset." He was sobbing with something like relief. Maddie found it hard to reconcile this man who was threatening to jump off the roof with the reasonable suggestions he made about what a woman needed after being raped.

He asked her for a piece of paper and pencil to scribble his fiancée's name and telephone number on as well as his own. Maddie rummaged through her handbag, unearthing her eyeglass case, wallet, comb, tissues, keys until she uncovered a loose receipt for articles she had recently bought at CVS. She carefully unfolded the paper, smoothed it out against her thigh and gave it to Pete. He wrote down the information on the back and returned it to her. She put it in her pocket. He put his hand forward to shake on it. Jack moved closer. Maddie shook Pete's hand.

"I'm coming over. OK?" Jack asked. Pete nodded in the gloom and the three of them walked off the roof and down the stairs.

As Jack opened the door to let Maddie and Pete through, the news photographer took a photo of them. The cops rushed forward. "Go easy on him, please. He never intended to jump and he's sorry for the drama he caused. He was distraught about his fiancée," Maddie said.

The reporter rushed over to her. "Any comment?"

"Only that this man is suffering terribly because of what his fiancée has been through. He wants me to help women like her who don't know where to turn." Maddie felt she couldn't say more. She thought people would deduce from what she said a number of situations that might be the problem. Pete wanted privacy. She had respected that. The reporter wanted more. Maddie simply answered, "I've pledged myself to help him. No further comment," and with that stepped into the back of the police car.

A cop drove Maddie and Jack home. Maddie sat back and thought about this poor man and his fiancée. No one should have to go through such an event alone. Despite Pete's harebrained scheme, Maddie felt sorry for him—and his fiancée. His distress had made him act like a madman. She hoped she'd be in a position to help.

The next morning the state newspaper had a photo of Maddie on the front page, coming out of the building, walking next to Pete. "Well," she said, "he got his publicity."

"And he got you some publicity too."

As Maddie read the accompanying story in the *Providence Journal*, she began to reflect on the meaning of her city's name. Roger Williams founded Providence as a refuge. For him, government derived its power from its citizens. We'll have to wait and see, Maddie mused, if Providence still practices that. After all, it was hardly a stretch to think that government should work for *all* its people, men and women alike.

LUISA

ROME, APRIL 1944

Luisa was back on the streets of Rome, biking along with her "laundry." She was transporting weapons to some partisans. As she approached a stop light, some German soldiers drew up beside her. She looked straight ahead.

"*Fräulein*," one said, "Aren't you the girl who delivers laundry for her mother?"

"Yes," she answered, looking him in the eye. It was the same soldier she had met when she first started deliveries for the partisans. It seemed like a lifetime ago. She didn't recognize the other Germans, except for the one in the back that she could see was smiling—more like leering—at her. He sat next to another soldier, slumped against the back seat.

The driver got out of his car and walked over to her. "How are you?"

"Fine. And how are you?" She maintained her composure.

"Oh, I've been busy. It's nice to see you again."

"Thank you." She immediately thought about what he was busy at: rounding up Jews.

"How are things going for you? You look a little thinner than when we first met."

"I've had a little cold and lost my appetite. But I'm fine."

"I'm sorry to hear about your cold. I'll get you some good tea for that and how about some sugar?"

She tried not to glare at him. She was outraged that he could get sugar. "Oh, it's really nothing. Just a little sniffle. I'm really fine.

Please don't bother yourself."

"No, no. I insist. Meet me here next Tuesday afternoon at five o'clock and I'll bring you some tea and sugar and I'll see what else I can scare up."

"You're too kind but it really isn't necessary. My mother will be worried about me out at that time of day when it's already getting dark."

"Tell her for me that there's no reason to be worried. I'll take good care of you." With that, he drove off. Luisa was shaking with anger and fear. What would he want from her in return?

Instead of making her drop of the two guns she was supposed to deliver, she turned her bike around and headed home along the same road she had taken to get there. She parked her bike, emptied the basket, and went inside to help her mother prepare supper, if that's what you could call it.

The next day she walked towards Antonio's, her partisan contact. She returned the guns, which she had put in a school bag.

"What is he going to want from me? You know I have nothing to give him and these Germans, sniffing all around, only want girls' bodies."

"I'll send a couple, a man and a woman on motorcycles, so that they don't arouse any suspicions, to be in the area near you. It's best to go to meet him so that he doesn't go hunting for you. These soldiers insist upon being obeyed. My guys will have these two guns with them and I'll get them a grenade as well. So stop worrying."

But Luisa couldn't stop worrying. She had another one of her fearful dreams that night. She was on a train going east. She was crowded into a boxcar with many other people. No air circulated. Everyone was moaning and crying out for water. The train kept going faster and faster. It shuddered on the tracks, forcing everyone helter-skelter against each other and against its walls. It streaked through the night until it went off the track. People were thrown through the roof. When they landed, they miraculously got up and ran, but Luisa couldn't move. She lay there until a German soldier stood over her with his gun pointing at her. She heard a boom in the distance and woke up.

The sounds of thunder moved nearer and nearer. Luisa heard another loud clap. She sat up and rubbed her eyes. Her heart raced. "The Lord is my shepherd. I shall not want," she chanted until her heartbeat returned to normal.

The next Tuesday, she dressed carefully. She wore a turtleneck sweater and a pair of old work pants she had stashed away in the back of her closet, and started out to meet the German. She pedaled listlessly, forcing herself to keep moving forward. She wasn't sure that Antonio's advice to meet him was the best, but she was so upset she couldn't think straight. She reassured herself by deciding that Antonio had more experience than she and that his was the best course of action to take.

Pedestrians on the street were thinning out on this drizzly day. All she noticed was the gloom and damp, which settled on her bones. She put more energy into her pedaling, downcast as she arrived at the meeting spot. The street was empty. The walls of the buildings on either side were stained by the grime of years. In the distance she made out a couple standing alongside their motorcycles. Her panic receded a bit. She wiped her brow with her coat sleeve. Then she heard a car motor. She turned to see the German soldier, smiling from the driver's seat. The same leering soldier sat in the back, again with the same third soldier accompanying them.

"Good evening, *Fräulein*. How are you?" The driver greeted her cheerfully and didn't even wait for a response. He got out of his car, all six feet of him, standing tall. "Look what I was able to get for you: tea and sugar as I said, but also coffee—real coffee—and flour." He rummaged in the back seat of the car. He turned back to her and held up each item: the tea, the sugar, the coffee and the flour, then plunked it all in a large bag. He looked so satisfied with himself.

Luisa was overcome with emotion, the emotion of anger, that he had access to all of that while Italians were starving, *dying* of starvation. She steadied her voice as she responded.

"That's really much too much. I can't accept it all. It's very kind of you, but—"

"Don't be silly. Who else can I give it to except you, my friend?"

Friend? Luisa thought. She wanted to scream, scream "murderer," grab him by the throat and squeeze with all her might. He sauntered over to her, like he had all the time in the world and offered her the bag. Luisa didn't move.

"Here. Take it. I insist." He shoved the bag into her hand. Luisa had no choice but to accept it.

"You're very kind. Your mother must be very proud to have such a thoughtful son." She thought that if she mentioned his mother, he might be embarrassed enough to do nothing untoward and be on his way.

"Yes, and I have a wonderful sister too. I miss her very much," he admitted.

Luisa gazed at him for a long time. She was speechless. She hadn't expected such a humane expression from him. She didn't know what to make of it. She took the bag, expressed her thanks and turned to leave.

"When will I see you again?"

She stayed quiet for a moment. "Oh, I'm sure we'll meet again—sometime."

"When is your next delivery of laundry, *Fräulein*?"

"I won't know until my mother tells me. It's not every day that she has work."

"Well, why don't we meet here again next Tuesday at the same time. We'll see what food I can scrounge up for you by then. Such a pretty *Fräulein* shouldn't be deprived . . . of anything."

Luisa shuddered, turned her bike, and left. This time she headed straight for Antonio's.

"He wants to meet me again next Tuesday. What shall I do?"

"You'd better meet him. I'm sure by now he's discovered where you live."

"How could he? He's never followed me home."

"Last time you met you said that you biked straight home. It wouldn't have been difficult for him to follow you at a distance without you even being aware of it."

"Wouldn't I have heard the motor of his car?"

"Do you really think you could pick out his motor from the other cars on the road? He could go as fast or as slow as he wanted and no driver would have dared to honk a horn at him. We'll follow the same scenario as last time. An armed couple will be nearby on motorcycles to help in an escape. OK?"

"Why can't you just put me in a safe house for a while until this blows over?

"Every safe house I know of is full up and more. The Germans have been ramping up the pressure. A lot is happening in the area. Things I can't talk about. Please, Luisa, don't fight me on this. Take my advice, please."

Her nerves were shot. She could see no other choice but to follow Antonio's orders.

ARTEMISIA

Rome, early 1600s

Today was a day that I had a lesson with Tassi. I wondered what he would be like. Would he have let go of his upset from the other day or had he held on to it? I hadn't dared to see Giorgio since then. Better to let sleeping dogs lie, as the saying goes. There was no need to push Tassi's face in it, though I felt resentful that I had to be the one to initiate the peace. I missed Giorgio's good nature.

He came through the door slowly, walking purposefully towards me.

"How are you today, Artemisia?" he asked, swirling his handkerchief about.

"I'm fine thank you, *maestro*. How are you?"

"I'm fine too and I'm glad to know that you've stopped seeing Giorgio."

How did he know that I hadn't seen Giorgio since their fight? In my mind, I certainly hadn't *stopped* seeing Giorgio. I just hadn't seen him *recently*. But I made no answer and swallowed my anger. Tassi was maddening and would exasperate a saint. I had never told him that I wouldn't see Giorgio ever again. I turned to my easel and picked up my palette and brushes. "Shall we begin today's lesson, *maestro?*"

"*Certo*. We'll start *today's* lesson," he answered and with that he swung me around and started yelling, "No more painting. No more painting." He threw my palette and brushes on the floor. I grabbed a knife to protect myself and slashed at him in several places. He grabbed the knife out of my hand. Then he pushed his handkerchief into my mouth, grabbed me by the throat, pushed me to the floor and forced his knee between my thighs so that I had no recourse but to open my legs. He rammed himself into me with such force that blood was everywhere.

"That's the best lesson I could give you. Don't you ever speak to me again the way you spoke to me the other day." He stalked out of the studio.

I must have lost consciousness for a moment. I lay on the cold floor for a very long time, moaning. My body ached all over. All sorts of thoughts went through my head. How could a man, specifically Tassi, be so despicable, so cruel? He must have known that I was a virgin and yet he set out to ruin my life because of his pride. What about *my* honor? He had relegated me to a convent. That was my only choice. Or he could marry me. What a choice that was! And yet at the moment that was preferable to life in a convent, singing, praying and cleaning all day long with no right to step outside its boundaries. I couldn't see straight. Which was worse? They both seemed like a death sentence.

Then it occurred to me: where was Tuzia who was supposed to chaperone me? She always sat at the back of the studio but she wasn't there today. Why not? I wondered.

I rolled over and knelt on all fours, like a beaten dog. I remained there a while, tugged the handkerchief from my mouth, panting and crying, mucus running down my face, ultimately mixing with the blood on the floor. I attempted to rise, but I fell forward into all that muck and started yelling, "I can't get up. I can't get up. Help me." But no one came. Where was Tuzia?

"Tuzia, Tuzia," I called. "Where are you, Tuzia?"

I knew my father was out, seeing to a possible commission from a powerful priest.

GIULIA and LUISA

Rome, March 1944

Luisa had no choice but to tell Giulia what had transpired. She omitted any mention of partisan activity and just said that a German soldier had come up to her and offered her food: tea, real coffee, sugar and flour. She tried to resist accepting it, but he had been adamant. She gave the food to her mother. She certainly wasn't going to make the food go to waste.

"Mamma, I'm so afraid of what he's going to ask of me in return for the food."

"Of course. Let me think a minute." She sat with her face in her hands, looking down at the table. This was a serious situation and she needed to be clever and quick in finding a solution. But nothing was coming to her. How she wished that Matteo were here to help. He was a clever boy. Then it came to her.

"You remember Antonio, Matteo's friend?"

Luisa nodded, staring at her mother, but saying nothing.

"He had helped find a safe house in the countryside to hide Matteo. I know how to get in touch with Antonio again. I'll do that first thing tomorrow and see what he says. Perhaps we can find a safe house for you too. In the meantime, I don't want you to leave the house. Do you understand?"

"But what if Antonio doesn't know of any safe houses that have openings?"

"Then we'll see if we can get in touch with Matteo and you'll hide with him or perhaps you could go to the Alps and hide in Nonno and Nonna's village."

"But if I were in their village, wouldn't it put them at risk? I don't think we should involve them."

"Hm-m, you may be right—but maybe not. Let me talk to Antonio and see what his suggestions are."

Luisa nodded agreement. It sounded like the place to begin. She was stupefied. Why hadn't Antonio suggested hiding out when all this had first started, instead of having her meet with the soldier? Surely, he could have found *some* place for her to hide. Was he so frazzled that he couldn't put this solution in place? Was he under such pressure that he didn't want to lose a courier? As Luisa thought more about it, she realized that a couple with guns following her on motorcycles for their escape was too out in the open and bound to cause further problems. Why hadn't she challenged Antonio more about his "solution"?

First thing the next morning, Giulia made contact with the person who knew where Antonio was, to see what she could arrange.

Early that evening Giulia left to meet Antonio. Luisa stayed inside as her mother had directed. She paced the floor as she waited for her mother to return. Angry thoughts whirled in her head. Didn't Antonio think she was worth saving by any means necessary? He didn't seem to take the threat seriously enough. Did he have such faith in Luisa's ability to get out of any scrape, as she *had* proven, that he didn't take this latest threat seriously? Her pacing took on greater and greater speed and frenzy. She heard someone turning the knob of the front door. Expecting to see her mother, she raced to it and opened it.

Instead, it was the German soldier she had seen leering at her in the back seat of the jeep. She gasped. She tried to shut the door, but he planted his foot in the opening, blocking her attempt. He held a bottle of schnapps in his meaty hand and pushed his way in. He was drunk.

"I thought you and I would have a private little party. Have some schnapps." He thrust the bottle at her. Luisa stood there frozen.

"Come on. Don't just stand there like a dummy, get us some

glasses." He pushed her towards the kitchen cupboards.

Luisa couldn't think straight. She tried to calm herself as she moved towards the cupboards. She took down two small glasses and placed them on the table, while she searched for something to hit him with.

He pushed the glasses aside. "Find us two big glasses to drink from. Not these puny little things, suited for children."

"Maybe you've had enough of that already? I'm not really a drinker of hard liquor. How about we have some wine instead?"

"No. I'm a soldier and this is what I like. You'll like it too." He shoved her aside and looked for large glasses while Luisa focused on finding something with which to protect herself. She saw a knife resting on the cutting board. She shuffled slowly towards it.

The soldier grabbed her by the arm before she could reach the knife. "Come 'ere," he slurred. "I found the right glasses." He banged them down on the kitchen table.

"Come 'ere," he repeated. "Can't you give your knight in shining armor a little kiss for finding the right size glasses? We're going to have so much fun." He pulled her to him and smothered her mouth with wet kisses. Luisa found him repulsive. The more she tried to pull away from him the more he clutched her to him.

"Don't be like that, coy with me. I know you want it." He tugged at her blouse, ripping it as he pulled it off her. His hands were up her skirt and into her pants. Luisa struggled to get free of him, but he was so much stronger than she. She began to shout, but he punched her in the mouth. Blood gushed out. "Oh, you're a tiger all right. I like a woman with some vim and vinegar to her." He laughed wildly. Luisa moaned. Then with one hand, he held her hands behind her back. Next, he lowered his pants, ripped her underpants off and thrust himself into her. Luisa sank to the floor. He took one last slug of the schnapps and threw the bottle of liquor on top of her, both cursing her and laughing as he stumbled to the door and down the stairs. Luisa lay there motionless.

Her upstairs neighbor sank into the shadows as the German

exited the apartment. When she no longer heard his footsteps on the stairs, she entered. She scanned the room but saw no one. She listened for any noise. Hearing nothing, she entered the kitchen.

"Luisa," she gasped. She knelt down beside the girl and touched her forehead. Luisa was slightly warm. She hurried into the bathroom and wet a towel. Back in the kitchen, she placed the cold towel on Luisa's forehead and lifted her head slightly. Luisa stirred. "It's all right, Luisa. Everything's going to be all right."

Luisa fluttered her eyelids. She opened her eyes. A wild look greeted Laura's gaze. Luisa glared unseeingly at Laura, but said nothing. She held the girl in her arms, murmuring as she stroked Luisa's hair, "It's all going to be all right," even though she didn't believe a word of it. What monster could do such a thing to such an innocent girl? Luisa continued to glare into empty space. Then she started struggling to get out of Laura's arms. She twisted this way and that. Laura put her arms around Luisa's waist and helped her get up. She sat Luisa down in a kitchen chair. Luisa slumped over.

"Come," Laura said, "let me put you to bed." Luisa leaned on Laura as the two of them shuffled towards her bedroom. She helped Luisa lie down, covered her with a blanket, and just as Giulia entered the apartment, Laura walked into the front room.

"Laura, hello. I didn't expect to see you here." Giulia looked around the room. "Is everything all right?"

"Better sit down. Both of us."

"What's the matter?" Giulia sat down and then got up again. She was beginning to panic. "What's the matter?" she asked. "For heaven's sake, Laura, tell me what's happened?"

Laura held Giulia's hands in her own and patted them. "A few minutes ago, I thought I heard a scream coming from your apartment. I came downstairs and saw a soldier leaving the apartment. He left the door open so I came in." Laura stopped to give Giulia time to take this in as well as to give herself time to figure out the best way to tell Giulia how she found Luisa.

"Yes, yes?"

"And I found Luisa on the floor with her clothes all askew."

"*Dio mio.*" Giulia jumped up. "Where is she?"

"She's lying down on her bed."

Giulia ran into the bedroom and let out a muffled scream. She felt as if she had been punched in the stomach. Her heart beat furiously. She thought her heart would fail her if she couldn't calm herself.

"Luisa, Luisa. It's Mamma. I'm here, sweetheart. I'm here." She grabbed at her daughter's hand and held it. Luisa turned her head to look at her mother. Tears gushed from her eyes. Giulia sat and cried along with her.

"Oh, Mamma," she finally said and then fainted.

The next morning, Giulia cleaned up. She threw out the clothes Luisa had been wearing the night before. Then she attempted to clean up Luisa. She heated some water and gently washed Luisa, who sat there and let her mother attend to her. When Giulia had finished, she wrapped Luisa in a large towel and helped her dress.

"How do you feel?"

"Terrible. Terribly violated. I don't know how I'm . . ." She broke down in tears again.

"I can only imagine, *cara mia*. It's all my fault, not getting back fast enough from Antonio's. I'll never forgive myself."

Luisa couldn't deal with her own ordeal. But she needed to help her mother too. Somehow, she couldn't do it; she was at war with her own emotions and with her feelings of compassion for her mother's suffering on her behalf. She breathed deeply and groaned. She felt desolate for not trusting herself and for listening to Antonio instead. She had been right in her instinctive reactions to events, such as when she had met the old man with his wife. Her hands were shaking. She had to get hold of herself if she were to survive. She forced herself to fold her hands together.

"What did Antonio say? About a safe house."

"He said there were a lot more Jews seeking hideouts because the Germans were getting more and more aggressive, but that he'd get back to us when he had something."

Luisa wrung her hands and tried to start thinking of a different solution.

Her mother's heart was broken. She held her daughter's body close to her. Eventually she said, "Antonio said that I should hide out with you. Since the Germans know where we live, I'm in danger too . . . of that soldier coming back here. . ." Giulia had heard that the Germans had hung a woman in Rome.

Luisa looked up. She rubbed her eyes in an attempt to dry her tears. "I guess that makes sense. I'm so sorry, Mamma." Luisa noted that her mother had aged during this ordeal. Wrinkles near her eyebrows had deepened and the lines on her face were more pronounced.

"You're sorry . . . You're sorry," her mother repeated as if in a trance. "I'm sorry. We're all sorry but you don't need to be sorry. It's the soldier who needs to be sorry. We just have to move on and get on with things."

Get on with things? Luisa thought. How could she do that? She wanted to kill that soldier, limb by limb. Better yet, she wanted to skin him alive. She wanted him to suffer as she had suffered, was suffering. She vowed that, somehow, she would prevail.

MADDIE

PROVIDENCE, SEPTEMBER 1978

Maddie needed to prepare for her class. Today she was to continue her presentation of women artists of the Renaissance. She had presented Sofonisba Anguissola's works during the last class. For today's class, she would introduce Artemisia Gentileschi's works. Compared to Artemisia's, Sofonisba's paintings were a walk in the park, most consisting of family portraits and benign scenes of well-to-do people.

Maddie hoped that her students wouldn't blanch at Artemisia's paintings. Would they find them brutal in their rendition of Judith's beheading of Holofernes? Or would they understand why she painted this scene over and over again? The first rendering of the painting shows Judith's servant and Judith with sword in hand, standing over Holofernes who is lying on a bed with sheets covered in blood. A great amount of blood drips down the bed and onto the floor. Judith is unflinching as she goes to work, cutting Holofernes's throat. Artemisia painted this just a year after Tassi raped her, a rape in which much blood was shed.

A year later, Artemisia painted Judith and her maid servant looking to the right, listening apprehensively to a noise in the darkness after having beheaded Holofernes. The servant carries Holofernes's head in a basket, lying on bloody sheets—those bloody sheets again. In 1625—fourteen years after the rape—she paints another "listening" scene with Judith and her servant, now looking to the left. Judith is no longer apprehensive, just attentive, nor is there much blood surrounding Holofernes. In this painting, Judith is in control and in command of the situation. She'll deal with whomever shows up. Maddie concludes that Artemisia has worked through a lot of the trauma from Tassi's rape of her—though it's still on her mind.

What Maddie finds interesting is that even before the rape, Artemisia painted works showing women in vulnerable situations. In the 1610 *Susanna and the Elders*, two men threaten Susanna. Unless she sleeps with them, they will spread false gossip about her. For Maddie, all this punctuates Artemisia's awareness of the weak place in society that women held. It was definitely on her mind.

Jack was coming over for dinner that night and Maddie was eager to talk to him about the events of the other evening.

"Jack," she said, "I can't stop thinking about Pete and his fiancée. That poor girl—and poor Pete."

"I know what you mean, Maddie. It's been on my mind too. They're both really suffering. And it's no wonder."

"I was thinking about what Pete said about a 'safe' house, so to speak, where rape victims could go for some support and as a safe place for them to stay immediately after."

"If you're elected, that's what you could lobby the legislature for."

"*If* I'm elected. One story in a newspaper about me doesn't a garden make. I'm not saying that I don't appreciate the coverage I got from speaking to Pete on the rooftop, but it just puts my name out once. A lot of readers won't even know that I'm their candidate for the state senate. My candidacy was a long shot to begin with and that hasn't changed. My focus now is on making a decent showing with maybe some clout to influence legislators."

"I see what you mean. It's a good way to go."

"My hope is that after the election, I'll be able to speak to some key legislators about such a home. The better I do, the better my chances of their acting on it. I've also been thinking about one of the artists I presented in class."

"Which one?"

"Artemisia Gentileschi. Her art teacher raped her and then she began painting pictures of Judith beheading Holofernes, her people's enemy, a number of times. I think that's how she healed herself. The first painting is full of blood on the sheets where Holofernes lies dead. Judith is poised over him; her arm is at his throat and she's resolute as she severs his head from his body. Revenge is apparent. She also does other paintings of Judith with her maidservant. They hear a noise after they've killed Holofernes and they stop to see who's coming. Again, there's a lot of blood, and Judith is anxious about who's coming, but, in the *later* painting of the same subject, as she listens, she's no longer worried about being caught; she's now in control, and there's not a lot of blood. She'll handle whoever comes upon them. In other words, the reduction of the blood means that Artemisia's getting over all the blood spilled when she was raped. Revenge is less important to her now and Judith's lack of anxiety about someone approaching means that Artemisia no longer feels the loss of control that rape victims usually feel. So, she's healing herself through her art."

"Wow. You're really on to something."

"I also think that a lot of her paintings were comments about women's place in society. Women had a weak place to no place in society, no rights. For example, to me her Penitent Magdalen's face suggests that Magdalen is thinking that she's not the only one to have sinned. There were men involved in her sin, too. Her brow is creased. She looks into the distance, suggesting that she is meditating on what she did—with men—for which she has remorse. It seems to me that she's asking for understanding, reminding us that there were partners in her sin. Then there's the ancient Roman Lucretia, who's supposed to kill herself because she's been dishonored by being raped and has brought dishonor to her family. She sure looks to me like she's questioning that belief as she holds the sword. She's not rushing to kill herself because she's troubled by the logic of having to kill *herself* to restore her honor. The sword is tilted very slightly towards her, but she's frozen from any movement to stab herself. The sword's mainly pointing up and away from her. Her head is bent back, a questioning expression on her face. Instead, she's reasoning:

I should kill myself because a man committed a crime against me? That's definitely what she's saying to me in that painting."

"It sure does sound like Artemisia was healing herself through her art and that she shows Lucretia doing some good thinking."

"And then by the 1640s, about thirty years after her rape, she has some fun with her painting of *Corisca and the Satyr*. We're shown a dark cloudy background. The satyr is chasing Corisca to rape her. He grabs for her hair and he ends up with her wig while she escapes from his grasp."

"That's one way to avoid rape!"

"I think that painting shows that Artemisia has put the rape behind her. She's as free as Corisca. As a matter of fact, Corisca is in control of the situation. She's put one over on the satyr. Artemisia shows the woman having power, not the satyr. She's outsmarted him with her intellect. Just as Artemisia's intellect—and talent—have shown her the way past her rape. Each person has to find her own way to overcome the effects of a rape."

"That must be really hard to do."

"But it must be done so that it doesn't affect the woman for the rest of her life. Artemisia may have started that healing process when she insisted on taking her rapist to trial for his crime."

"Brave woman," Jack said. "A lot of women even today don't want to go down that path."

"Can you blame them? Another time I'll tell you what happened to Artemisia at her trial."

ARTEMISIA

ROME, EARLY 1600S

Tuzia never showed up that awful day. Father finally came back from his meeting with the priest to find me still lying on the floor in disarray amidst much blood.

"Artemisia," he yelled, "what's happened? How are you?"

I could barely talk. My throat was dry and every bone in my body ached. I still clenched Tassi's handkerchief in my hand and heaved it in anger as far away from me as I could. All I wanted to do was lie there and think. Think about what I would do to Tassi if I ever saw him again. Although I certainly didn't want to see him, I wanted to punish him, but how could I do that without seeing him? That was a conundrum that I had no answer for. My brain swirled around in useless thoughts and misdirected logic. The least of the things that I wanted to do to him was to push his head under water while I kicked him between his legs. Then I wanted to gouge out his eyes so that he could never paint again.

It seemed to me that those measures *might* be equal to the harm he had done me. My choices in what I could do in my life had been taken away from me. I had been dishonored or as the gossips might say, I was "damaged goods." No one would want to marry me. The convent—I shuddered at the thought—was all I was good for. I went back to thinking of the ways I could hurt Tassi. My hate for him at that moment almost suffocated me. I grabbed at my throat and stifled a scream.

Father repeated his question. I tried to breath normally. I was a little more successful this time in getting up. I leaned back on my forearms and told him what had happened. His face contorted and his eyes became watery.

"What can we do, Father?" I whispered.

"We'll see," he said. "We'll see."

Father helped me up and called for Tuzia, but there was no response. I assured him that I could clean myself up. I left Father pacing back and forth in my studio, his head down, deep in thought. I commenced to clean myself but it was a more difficult task that I had imagined. Just lifting sufficient water to pour into the basin to wash was almost more than I could endure. I scrubbed at my body in an attempt to get Tassi's odor off me until my skin turned red. I could still feel his hands on me. I sat down on my bed and cried. How long I sat there, I have no idea. I threw on some clothes and went to look for Father.

He was still in my studio, deep in thought. As I entered, he looked up. "He must marry you."

I stared at Father, but said nothing.

"He must marry you," Father repeated.

"Do you really think I want to marry him, Father?" I stifled a scream.

Father studied me. "Do you want to go into a convent then?" He actually thought he was offering me an alternative.

"Let's not rush into making a decision," I said, not much above a whisper.

Soon everyone in town heard about what had happened. Tuzia gave some excuse for not being at her usual seat in my studio. Something about her receiving a message from her sister to come right away because one of her children was sick and she needed Tuzia's help. I didn't believe her for a minute.

Giorgio, dear Giorgio, came by too.

"How are you, Artemisia?" he said, his brow wrinkled in worry.

"I'm all right now, Giorgio. I've had some time for my body to heal and my mind is thinking more clearly now too."

"I'm glad to hear that, Artemisia. I was bereft when I heard the news . . . What are you going to do?" he asked.

"I'm just beginning to think about that, Giorgio."

"Are you going to marry him?"

"Absolutely not."

Giorgio looked at me for a long time. So long that I was beginning to feel uncomfortable. Would he too think of me as damaged goods?

"Will you marry me, Artemisia?"

I ran towards him. "Oh, Giorgio. That's the most beautiful thing that anyone could say to me right now. You've always been such a good friend to me. But I think that's not such a good idea for you. You'd only be criticized and spoken poorly of in the neighborhood for marrying a woman who has been dishonored. But I'll always be grateful to you for your beautiful offer and your loyalty to me."

He took off his hat and moved it around in his hands, round and round. His face showed nothing. Then he turned and walked away slowly.

"Wait," I called. He stopped but didn't turn. "Oh, Giorgio," I said and ran into my studio, sobbing at having such a loyal friend, whom I could not accept in marriage.

Father and I had been discussing how we should proceed for a long time. I decided it was time to make a decision and take action, come what may.

LUISA

Rome, May 1944

Luisa soon learned why Antonio hadn't focused as carefully as she wanted him to on her situation. In January, American spies had infiltrated Rome to prepare for the invasion of Anzio. Many meetings followed and many arrangements had to be made. Moving weapons and people were the least of it. Complicated logistics needed to be planned and implemented. Antonio attended many meetings with the National Liberation Committee about the forthcoming event. She understood that she was a small cog in a much larger, and more important, undertaking. Although she forgave Antonio for not giving her his full attention, she continued to have unsettling dreams.

One of them took place in a part of Rome Luisa didn't recognize, yet at the same time she knew the address of one of the buildings, which was demolished and yet still standing and partly intact. It was at 145 Via Tasso, the Gestapo headquarters, where people were tortured. In her dream, she walked up some stairs and proceeded along an outside platform, where she walked on bodies that were absolutely flat, one-dimensional. She shuddered and then she went downstairs again. A ceremony was under way. A man with a huge chin and tiny mustache was the center of attention. She saw a big fire in the piazza with people cheering. She found her way home meeting with some tourists who were not really tourists. With the screech of a train's whistle, Luisa awoke.

It was easy enough for Luisa to figure out the meaning of her dream—Hitler and Mussolini publicly meeting, the Gestapo and torture, book burnings, spies, trains filled with Jews—but then she let it go. What was the point? she thought. The reality was that the Germans were tightening the noose on Italians and Jews. Many Italians were answering back with increased partisan activity, all of which inflamed the Germans more. More graffiti against Hitler and Mussolini was appearing on walls. Nuns in villages were delivering messages, warning Jews when the Germans were coming. Luisa heard of one nun who ran a school in which she hid Jewish children. When safe, the nun would take the children skiing to give them something that approximated a normal childhood in spite of what was happening.

Rumors swirled about the Anzio invasion. Anzio was near enough to Rome to give people hope, but they had heard nothing further about the invasion since January, only rumors, different rumors each day of the week. It was enough to drive people crazy. If Allies could infiltrate spies into Rome, why couldn't they do something with the troops in Anzio? she wondered. Why hadn't they moved beyond Anzio?

The Italians hadn't learned about all the difficulties connected with the Anzio landing: the low-lying marshlands with no vegetation, causing the Allied trenches to fill with water; German Field Marshal Kesserling taking advantage of American Major General Lucas's urging caution along with his decision to dig in—all these factors contributed to the stalemate at Anzio. And then there was the rumor about some G.I.s in a jeep, riding into Rome to find out what the Germans were up to, finding the city totally quiet. When the G.I.s informed their commander of that, he did nothing! Was this a war or a ping-pong game gone eerily awry?

Luisa continued to dwell on the rape. She was so angry she could think of little else than ways of punishing the soldier, even though she knew her thinking was no more than a pipe dream. She tried to remain calm while Antonio found a place where she and her mother could safely hide. Finding such a place seemed to get more and more difficult as each day passed. In the meantime, she and her mother sat in their apartment. Their neighbor Laura helped out by getting them food. But that had become a major undertaking with food rationing and the price of pasta alone tripled since the war began.

Despite themselves, Mother and daughter dipped into the small trove of food that the German had given Luisa. They found it was a mixed blessing: on the one hand, it reminded Luisa of what she had been through; on the other hand, it sustained them. They shared the real coffee and sugar with Laura. It was the least they could do. Laura couldn't help being ecstatic over tasting real coffee again and having the luxury of adding sugar to it, though she too was reminded of Luisa's sufferings. She had known Luisa since she was a little girl, eagerly starting her first day at school, skipping along, her hair flying all about as she held her mother's hand. It was hard for Laura to see her suffering so now. They all did the best they could under very trying circumstances. They had no alternative but to play a waiting game—a little like the Anzio situation, they thought ruefully.

MADDIE

PROVIDENCE, SEPTEMBER 1978

The next week, Maddie met with Deedee. She learned an interesting piece of information: the reason the state representative was so eager to have someone run against the Senate Minority Leader was because Maddie's opponent, that very same Senate Minority Leader, had put someone up against the representative during the previous election, and now the representative was playing payback, a simple game of revenge.

"That's so interesting, Dee. Why am I not surprised? Campaigning is hard and I'm sure elected officials want to avoid it at all costs and just swim along in their offices."

"It may be a bit confusing, but basically it's about revenge, a prime tool of politicians to thump their chests and retain their aura of power. Listen, I've arranged for us to meet with an arts group. It would be good for you to make contact with them. It's important to get specific groups supporting you. It gets people involved and more certain of voting on the actual day."

"OK. Sounds good. Thanks, Dee."

"Hey, I'm glad to help any way I can. Just let me know."

Dee had arranged for Maddie to meet with the arts group in a private side room at Camille's Roman Gardens, an old-time restaurant in Providence. It had a great reputation. Maddie already knew what she would order as an appetizer, the eel. She hoped it was still on the menu. She doubted that many people were into eel. She even wondered how she had come to love it so. As they say, "There's no accounting for taste."

Leaving the parking lot of the restaurant, she met a state representative who had become friendly with her. Maddie knew his sister from church.

"Hi, Maddie," he greeted her. "Where are you off to?"

"Going to meet some constituents. And you?"

"Same thing."

They laughed. "It's all consuming, isn't it?"

"I'm afraid so. So, how's it going?"

"Well, I'm trying my hardest. But it's a slog."

"I know what you mean. The campaigning's the worst part. I had to try—and campaign—four times before I got elected."

"Four times!" Maddie almost screamed the words. That was three too many for her. This would be her one campaign. When she went into this, she had thought she'd be learning what the issues of importance were to her constituents, their worries and concerns. She *was* getting out of it some of what she wanted, that she was capable of more than her profession and that she might be able to influence legislation. She had been teaching a long time. She thought of herself as a very good teacher and her evaluations seconded that. Ironically, that gave her the confidence to try something new. But what she needed right now was to *know* that she was capable of other things. She couldn't imagine doing this three more times. But who knows? Once you catch the bug ... Somehow, she doubted that she had.

Six leaders, each representing one group of artists working in the same building, were gathered around a dining table at the restaurant. It was set for eight places. Dee sat at one end of the table and, when she arrived, Maddie at the other.

Introductions were made all around and then Maddie asked if the artists had any ideas that they'd like to promote for legislation. A gnarly man with bright eyes was the first to speak up.

"We thought that the best thing that the state could do for us is set aside a small percentage from taxes to buy public art: put sculptures in squares and paintings in libraries, for example. It not only helps us artists by buying our works, but it also gives Providence a certain level of sophistication. It increases tourism," he added earnestly, "which brings money into the economy. The money given to us, in a way, is returned through the money that increased tourism brings."

Maddie was impressed. They had certainly done their homework and come up with an interesting proposal. Before she could comment, the waiter came to take their order.

When Maddie ordered the eel as her first course, the artists all looked up from their menus. A woman with frizzy hair said, "You're adventurous. I hope you'll be as adventurous when it comes to art."

"I intend to be." Maddie laughed. "I don't know if *you* know, but I teach art history at the community college so I'm very open to any of your suggestions. And I have some thoughts about something else that I'd like to run past you if you wouldn't mind."

Maddie first asked them to honor the privacy that Pete wanted and, when they agreed, she told them about him and his fiancée. One of the women chimed in, "Oh yes, I saw your photo in the paper, but didn't read the story."

"Well, his fiancée had been raped and all she did was cry and he was beside himself. He wants me to put in legislation to establish a safe house for victims of rape. I think it's something that's really needed and hope that you'll support me in this.

"Even today, women are unwilling to come forward and press charges against the men who raped them. They fear the publicity that a trial would bring and all the memories it would stir up. I'm afraid to say that attitudes haven't changed much in almost four hundred years."

"Oh, come now," the gnarly man protested. "Surely things are better now than they were in the seventeenth century."

"Not really. How many women have the courage of an Artemisia Gentileschi, who insisted on bringing her rapist to trial?"

The table remained quiet. Maddie allowed the pause to continue while everyone ordered their meals.

When everyone had finished ordering, Maddie let her question hang in the air and turned back to the subject that had brought the artists here in the first place. "I think you have a strong proposal and a good rationale for it, what with money going out *and* money coming back in. That's important. To be able to give something back when you get something. I'd be extremely happy to promote this *if* I'm elected."

"And that's where you people come in," Dee said. "You need to help us get Maddie's name out among your friends, make sure they vote and support her on the house for rape victims."

"Of course."

Dee continued. "Can you set up a phone chain on election day, where you call your voters, to urge them to go vote? People get busy with other things. They get lazy . . ."

"We'll have to figure out how to do that, but I think it's possible. Each building, where our studios are, could have a captain. Maybe better than a phone chain, the captain could go door to door in his or her building. We all know each other. If the person's not home, we could leave a note. How does that sound? Telephoning seems more complicated to me, the way we're set up."

"Pretty good." Dee had to admit, "and we can give you some campaign literature to hand out." With that done, they set themselves to do some real eating.

ARTEMISIA

ROME, EARLY 1600S

Despite my protests, Father had approached Tassi about marrying me. Father confided in me that Tassi practically laughed in his face and said, "Why would I want to do that?"

"Because you've dishonored her," Father cried, "and if you don't marry her, no one else will. Do you want her to end up in a convent?"

"Aren't you being a little dramatic? I'm sure her little model boyfriend would want to marry her."

"Don't be ridiculous. It's you who must marry her."

"Get it through your head. I'm not marrying your daughter or anybody else."

As far as I was concerned the convent was not a choice and I told Father so. And it was there and then that I made my decision. "I want to take Tassi to court."

My statement threw Father into a long silence. Finally, he asked, "What do you think you'd accomplish by that? More notoriety? How would that help you?"

"I don't care about more notoriety. Could it be any worse that it is now? Gossips all over Rome are chattering about it. Does Tassi worry about notoriety? He probably preens before others that he could take a woman like me. If I were a man, notoriety would be the last thing I'd worry about, just as Tassi doesn't seem to have a worry in the world."

Again, Father remained silent for a long time, even longer than before. He walked around the studio with his hand on his chin. I waited patiently while he meditated. I had come to a decision and I wasn't to be dissuaded. But I needed Father's agreement to proceed because I had no ability to accomplish what I was proposing. As a woman, I had no standing to bring any action before the court, but he did. I needed Father's help. I stayed silent too and paced around the studio, trying to think of ways to convince Father that we should go to court.

LUISA

Rome, May 1944

Luisa and her mother were getting anxious about Antonio's inability to find a safe house for them. At the same time, Luisa was dealing with the trauma she had been through with the German soldier. She found a bit of comfort in perusing her art books. For a few moments, at least, it took her mind off what had happened. And then she saw a volume with some of Artemisia Gentileschi's works displayed in it. She picked up the book and flipped through the pages. She started when she saw her two paintings of Judith beheading Holofernes. Although she was familiar with the works—she had seen the originals—the paintings had never struck her the way they struck her now. Luisa knew that Artemisia had been raped. When she saw the reproductions of the paintings with all the blood sinking into the sheets, she gasped.

"What is it, *cara mia?*" her mother asked.

"I just came across a painting by an artist who, like me, had been raped. The effects of that horror can be seen in her paintings. She's trying to externalize what she experienced to get over it, as if one can ever get over it." Luisa held up the book for her mother to see. Giulia gulped.

"I see what you mean." Her mother continued to study the paintings. She too noted all the blood dripping from the sheets that Holofernes's head was lying on. "Do you think drawing something about the rape would help you, Luisa?"

"I don't know, Mamma. I don't know. You know that drawing isn't my thing. I wish we weren't cooped up in our apartment. If only

I could go out and take some photos of what the Germans are doing. I know that would do me a world of good."

"Yes, I understand, but it's not a good idea for us to be outside, don't you agree?"

"But it's not a good idea for me to be inside brooding, either."

"I know what you mean, but it'll be soon that Antonio can get us into a safe house. I know it's hard, but we need to be patient."

"Mamma, you've been saying that for days and days now. I need to get out."

"Please, Luisa, don't do anything foolish and *that* would be foolish now."

"I've made up my mind, Mamma. If Artemisia could take her rapist to court, I can go outside. I'll be very careful, staying in the shadows and off the main streets. I've made my decision."

Her mother felt defeated. She knew Luisa was a *testa dura*, a hardhead, stubborn. When she made up her mind to do something, there was no changing it. Her indecisive young daughter had grown up to be a determined young woman. Giulia sighed. All she could do was pray that Luisa would take sufficient precautions to stay safe.

Luisa got up at dawn and prepared herself for her day. She skipped breakfast, hardly by choice—there was little food anyway—and then dressed herself in gray clothing so as not to attract attention. She slipped her camera into a medium-sized handbag, again not to attract attention, and quietly left the apartment, tiptoeing down the stairs.

When she arrived at the ground floor, she barely opened the door to the street. She pushed it open only wide enough for her to see outside. All was quiet. She slid along the wall of the building to the corner and turned down the small alley, hugging the wall and noting where she could hide if she needed to. She heard a car coming around the corner and hid behind some trash cans. A German soldier was at the wheel with other soldiers in the back. The driver wore a heavy field coat, perhaps a little too heavy for the day's weather. He had slicked back blond hair and a nose that Luisa could only describe as Roman. Thank God that he didn't have the eyes of a hawk and hadn't seen her. A wave of relief spread over Luisa. When they were gone, she continued on her way. She headed towards the Ghetto, the ancient Jewish quarter, to see what was happening there. All was quiet. Perhaps all the Jews had already been taken away—a discouraging thought.

Her foray continued to reap no results. She saw nothing that interested her, nothing worth exposing herself and her camera for. She walked home, feeling defeated, or was she defeating herself? Maybe there was something out there that she saw that she could photograph. But the scene that was always before her, of the drunken soldier, haunted her thoughts. Images of what had occurred arose unbidden.

Her mother noted her return but said nothing, thankful that nothing untoward had occurred. She idled through the art book that Luisa had been perusing until she happened upon a painting that showed Corisca escaping from the satyr. Giulia stared at the painting and smiled. She determined that Luisa should see it as soon as possible. That painting showed that Artemisia had found her way clear of the rape, because it showed that Corisca used her mind to outsmart the satyr. She had escaped from the satyr by wearing a wig when he had unsuccessfully grabbed at her hair. Giulia hoped Luisa would see the painting and learn from it, learn what Artemisia had learned. Luisa too could be in control of her life. She left the book on the kitchen table, open to that page, but said nothing.

MADDIE

PROVIDENCE, SEPTEMBER 1978

The next morning, Maddie was leafing through the newspaper. Buried inside was an article about her campaign. She read it eagerly. She was dismayed. The reporter had misrepresented her. She sat and thought about what she should do. She decided to go down to the newspaper offices on Fountain Street and talk to the reporter.

The newsroom was fairly busy at this early hour. She found the reporter's desk and introduced herself. He barely said hello. She talked to him in a conciliatory way about correcting the misrepresentation, but he flat-out refused. She was furious at his nerve, but left. She realized that the reporter always has the last word.

She called Dee. "Did you see the article in today's paper where I'm misrepresented?"

"I did. He's your opponent's reporter."

"What do you mean 'he's my opponent's reporter'?"

"It's clear as mud. He's on her side. He wants her to be re-elected. I wouldn't be at all surprised if she put him up to this."

Maddie sighed. "I went down to the paper and spoke to him, but he wouldn't change a thing."

Dee laughed. "At least you tried and confronted him. A reporter always has the last word, but you put him on notice that you'd track his articles for any further misrepresentations. You didn't take it sitting down. It's good for him to know that."

"Thanks for listening, Dee. I always appreciate your insights."

They hung up and Maddie started getting ready for her class. She put on her blue suit and matching pumps and sat down to make some notes about the points she wanted to make. One of the things she intended to do was to ask her class their reactions to Artemisia's situation.

Once everyone in her class had seated themselves and quieted down, Maddie started.

"So last session," she began, "we looked at paintings by Artemisia Gentileschi. After focusing on the *art* of her works, we discussed how her works seemed to mirror her psyche—her *Judith Slaying Holofernes, Susanna and the Elders, The Penitent Magdalen,* and *Corisca and the Satyr.* Do we all agree that she was using her paintings to heal herself from her rape?"

No one raised a hand to disagree. "OK, then," Maddie continued, "I'm curious about what you young women and men of today think about her choosing to go to trial. Was she wise to do that? Would you do that if you were in that situation? Has anything changed since Artemisia's time?"

Maddie was relieved; a number of students raised their hands. She always worried that her class might not find her questions worth discussing. She called on Jane Wilson who always had something to say.

"Given the outcome of the trial, I don't think it was worth going through what she went through. Nothing much has changed since then. It's still hard to go through something like that."

"Marcie, do you agree?"

"No, I don't. Artemisia took her rapist to trial more for her own sake to get past the rape and take back her own sense of herself as someone who had some power and control over her own life."

"But she didn't have any power in that society," Joe protested. "She had to get her father to bring Tassi to trial. It's not so different from today. Although a woman can bring her own case to court, she still has to contend with how people react to her. Do they believe her or do they right away dismiss what she says?"

"And taking Tassi to trial didn't change the choices she had, namely marriage or the convent. And it didn't change how people thought about her. She was still damaged goods, who no one wanted to marry," added Julie. "And although Tassi was found guilty, he suffered no consequences."

"We don't have thumbscrews today to see if a woman is telling the truth, but a woman is certainly put through the torture of the damned," Joan said.

"In what way, Joan?"

"In that she's not believed. But since we can't put her through the thumbscrews test, we malign her character and suggest that she's lying and that it was consensual. And they'll add to that smear by saying, 'Hey, if she was dressed the way she was, why was she surprised by what happened?'"

"How many agree that nothing much has changed for rape victims?"

A majority of hands went up to agree with Maddie's question. She sighed as she thought about the implications of that.

Maddie's thoughts turned to Pete and his fiancée. She needed to get back to them to find out how they were doing. She had found a therapist for Pete's fiancée. She hoped she had helped. Reluctantly, Maddie had to bring the class discussion to a close. It was certainly one of the livelier discussions that Maddie had introduced. Everyone seemed to have a point of view, but now she needed to move on and introduce them to other artists.

That evening right after supper, she called Pete.

"Hi, Pete. This is Maddie. How's everything going?"

"Thanks so much for calling, Maddie. My lawyer got me out on bail and he thinks that I have a good chance of having all charges dropped since I don't have any past offences."

"That's great news, Pete. I'm so happy to hear that. I was really worried about you. Once you get into the hands of the law, things can get twisted and stuck in bad places."

"I know. When they threw me into a waiting cell, a guy started talking to me. He had such a convoluted story—don't ask me to repeat it. It was too confusing for my brain—that I was seeing stars by the end of it. As he told me his story, he got more and more excited. I could relate to that, given my own crazy behavior that night. I was driven to distraction and couldn't see any way out of the maze that my mixed-up thinking had created."

"You certainly seem clear about where you're at now, Pete. I'm pleased because it proves my hunch about you being a basically decent person is correct."

"I wanna thank you for that belief in me. And I wanna tell you that my fiancée Alice called the therapist, who can't see her for another month. But, since Alice's willing to see the therapist, I hope she's beginning to look to putting all this behind her."

"Do you think she's not moving too fast? It takes a long time to get past such an event."

"I'm sure you're right. In the meantime, I wondered if you'd be willing to go see Alice. She was so close to her mother, who died about five years ago. She needs someone like you to just talk to."

Maddie sucked in her breath, surprised by the request. Since she was in this far already, she saw no alternative but to agree. She felt for Alice. That was for sure.

"Sure," she said. "We'll set up a time that's good for both of us."

Pete switched back to the other subject that was on his mind. "I wanted to ask you how I might help you in your election. Your win will be my win."

Maddie laughed in spite of herself. "I hadn't looked at it that way, but I get your point. My biggest need is getting my name out. A coffee at your house with your friends and neighbors invited is always helpful as long as they're in my district."

"I'm not sure I can do that at this time, what with Alice in a fragile condition, but I'd be willing to write postcards to my friends who live in your district and I'll follow up with a phone call."

A week later she and Pete went to see Alice, as promised. They entered Alice's apartment. Clothes were strewn everywhere. The floor could have used a good sweeping too. Shades were drawn over the windows. Half-filled glasses sat on a couple of side tables. Alice shrank into the sofa, her lank hair hanging unwashed and uncombed. She was so fragile that it was as if she didn't exist beyond the confines of the navy sofa. Maddie suppressed a gasp.

Alice tensed and then scowled as she stared at her visitors, she hunched up her shoulders, then slowly lowered them. A meekness that mirrored her feelings of abasement took over.

"Alice," Pete said, his mouth narrowed into an anxious line, almost talking through his teeth. "This is Maddie who I told you about. She's going to help us."

"Hello, Alice. You've been through the worst thing that can happen to a woman. I'm so very very sorry."

Alice scrutinized Maddie. Was this woman for real? she thought. I can't seem to breathe and I feel dead, she brooded. The least little noise has me up and running. But where am I running to in a four-room apartment? Where can I go so that I won't suffocate anymore? I'm desperate . . . so afraid.

"I'm here to help you in any way I can, Alice. Is there anything you can tell me so that I might be of help to you?"

Alice gazed at Maddie. Her voice was so soft and caring. She reminded her of her late mother—a woman who had died before her time. How Alice missed her, especially now when she needed her mother so badly. Who else would understand? Who else could she tell?

Alice looked into Maddie's eyes. She saw compassion there. Once a priest told her that expressing compassion for people who suffered was how good people could balance out the evil in the world. Alice wondered if the brutality she experienced had destroyed her soul. But she forced herself to begin to breathe in and out regularly. Maddie sat beside her, enveloping Alice's trembling hand in both of hers. She held it tight. Maddie felt a slight tightening of Alice's grip and squeezed back. Alice began to sob, tears streaming down her face without embarrassment. She began to talk about her rape. The words tumbled out faster than they could be digested: the force, the anonymity, the cruelty, the leering disregard of her humanity. Maddie put her arm around Alice's shoulder and hugged her, murmuring soothing words as she brushed her hair back from her face. The suffocation Alice felt was beginning to loosen.

When Alice finished talking, she was covered in perspiration, but she sat quietly and let Maddie stroke her head in a gentle movement. Alice breathed more regularly as time passed. Maddie was shocked into silence by what she heard. She wondered if another human being could hear such raw misery and survive, no less the victim. She wondered if she could survive. No words could describe the savage trauma that Alice had experienced and the emotions that followed. She looked at Pete, willing her face not to betray the anguish she felt. Nonetheless, she hurled herself up from the sofa. Pete moved to sit next to Alice, who let Pete hold her hand. Maddie tiptoed to the door and exited the building.

As Maddie drove home, she was reminded of an incident that occurred at a conference she was attending some eight years ago. A young man there suffering from alopecia, a disease that causes the loss of facial hair—no eyelashes, no eyebrows, etc.—had attended too. Though Maddie didn't know about the disease at the time, she never wanted to see anyone left out because they were different. So she approached him and started chatting. The second time she chatted with him, he stood very close to her and put his arm around her waist, all of which Maddie found very creepy. She stayed away from him for the remainder of the conference. Later an announcement was made that he had been asked to leave because he had assaulted a young woman. At that time, Maddie wasn't sure what the word "assaulted" meant. Was it a euphemism for rape? Had he raped her there in the bucolic setting of wildflowers and mountains? Maddie never found out, but the memory of her own experience of him never left her. It reminded her how lucky she had been to listen to her intuition.

Maddie slammed the brakes to stop at the red light. She put her face in her hands and gulped down tears. How unimaginably worse was rape itself? After hearing Alice talk about the event, Maddie was no closer to understanding what it was like. Maddie continued to think about the situation some more. She understood rape on an intellectual level and even on an emotional level, but she couldn't fathom the depths of insult to a woman's identity that it caused. Rape didn't only strike at a woman's sexuality, but rather it rubbed away at her soul. The car behind her honked its horn. The light had turned green. Maddie pulled herself together and continued on her way home.

ARTEMISIA

Rome, early 1600s

I think I have figured out how to get Father to initiate the trial against Tassi since, as a woman, I have no standing to bring the suit myself. Father is always concerned about money. The notoriety of my rape will reduce the price of my art and since he's my father, he can argue before the court that he has lost something, namely his daughter's earning power as well as my lesser worth as a marriageable daughter. There is also an issue of one of my works, which has gone missing. I'll have to convince Father that Tassi stole it, which is the truth. I only noticed it missing after my rape and since no one had been in the studio after that, he's my only suspect. He probably took it with him as he left. He's vindictive enough to think that raping me wasn't sufficient punishment.

"Father, I thought you would be eager to go to trial against Tassi," I began in my campaign to get him to initiate proceedings against the man. "After all, you've lost something: my earning power has been reduced and my suitability for marriage—by anyone—is gone. And I'm sure it was Tassi who took my painting after he raped me."

I could see Father mulling this over. He moved away from the easel with one of my unfinished paintings on it and looked at me as he tapped his chin. He stayed silent as he considered what I had said.

"I also need to consider, Artemisia, how the artistic community as a whole would look upon my taking Tassi to court. Would they be supportive of my action or would they think I was taking an unnecessary action against a fellow artist—an artist, I should remind you, who obtains numerous large commissions?"

I was taken aback by this argument, which I had not considered. Finally, I made a stab with my subsequent response since in Italy family was all. "Father, I do understand your hesitancy, but consider that the artistic community would honor you for supporting a family member who had been wronged. After all, the honor of the family is compromised as well. And then there's the stolen painting." I now thought it advisable to call it what it was, a *stolen* painting.

"Yes," Father replied hesitantly, "the artistic community would probably think of my family as of higher importance than anything else. Let me think about the implications of what you've said and I'll make a decision soon."

Days passed after this conversation and I became more and more agitated. The irony of my name, Artemisia, after the Greek goddess of chastity, Artemis, was not lost on me. Finally, Father called me before him. "I've made my decision, Artemisia. You've made some good points about why I should bring Tassi to court. On the one side, he has stolen a painting of mine as well as reducing my daughter's earning power and so in that respect he has stolen from me. He has also decreased your worth in terms of marriageable suitability since *he* won't marry you. On the other side, I have to consider the overall reaction of the artistic community and the added notoriety of a trial."

I held my breath as Father droned on. I wanted to yell at him, "What is your decision?" but I kept silent and bit my tongue.

"And so, considering all sides of the argument, and not making my decision lightly, but considering all the issues involved," he droned on in his pedantic way as he looked down at the floor, "I've made my decision." He stopped dramatically, raised his eyes to mine and announced, "I'll take Tassi to trial. He's taken something from me. He needs to compensate me for your lesser worth since he won't marry you. He has made you unsuitable to marry. He has committed a crime against the family honor. Not only did he take one of your paintings, but a part of my livelihood in that I won't get as much for your paintings now." He hurried on. "But, Artemisia, before I irrevocably agree to this, you must be aware of what will be expected of you. You'll be made to show that you're telling the truth, that you were not a willing person. Are you willing to go through all that?" he asked in a staccato voice.

I chafed at how he framed the trial. He framed it in terms of what money had been taken from him, not in what had been taken from me, my virginity, my choices in life. I ran towards him anyway to kiss him, something I rarely, if ever, did. He stiffened somewhat. "Oh, Father," I lied, "I knew you wouldn't let me down. Thank you, thank you. It's the right thing to do. Of course, I'll do whatever I have to, to prove our case against that monster."

"Well, we'll see," he huffed and with that he left the studio. The disappointment I felt at what motivated my father to take Tassi to trial was overwhelming. But then he had never shown much interest in me as a daughter, only in me as an artist who could help him get commissions—commissions through Tassi. Now I had to prepare for the ordeal. Little did I know what an ordeal it was to be.

LUISA

Rome, May 1944

Luisa sat in a chair near the window, which looked out over the front door of their apartment building. She was taken out of her useless reverie of her past horror when she heard a car stop in front of her building. She leaned over to see who was stopping at their address.

She gasped. "Mamma," she yelled to her mother who was in the kitchen, "come quick. It's the German soldier who gave me the food. Oh, my goodness," she moaned, "what does he want? Please God, let him not be stopping here to see me."

Giulia made little comforting noises to calm Luisa down. "Let's not jump to conclusions."

They heard his footsteps on the stairs, getting closer and closer. "We'll deal with whatever we have to when the time comes," her mother said, "and not before. Remember, 'A coward dies a thousand times before his death . . .'" A knock on their door cut the quote short.

"What shall we do?" Luisa whispered.

"We shall wait to see what develops." With that, her mother sat down and folded her hands.

"My deepest apologies," the German said at the closed door. Luisa's mouth dropped open. She looked at her mother. Giulia placed her finger over her lips.

"I hope you'll accept my apologies for the despicable behavior of my fellow soldier. I've placed him in confinement at the barracks," he began in a quiet, contrite whisper. "It's the very least I can do, but I needed you to know how terrible I feel . . . about everything." He choked on the last two words.

Giulia rose from her chair, walked towards Luisa and whispered into her ear. "I think we should let him in. He sounds very sincere to me. What do you think?"

"It could be a trick to commit more mayhem."

"I think we need to take him at his word. Did you hear how he choked on his last two words? Only a professional actor could do that . . . or someone who is totally sincere." She nodded to Luisa to open the door.

"If you insist, Mamma, but I'm against it," Luisa hissed back.

"I do insist. I think you need to start trusting people again, especially men." With that, Giulia strode to the door and opened it. Luisa gasped.

The soldier who had given her the food stood before them, stooped over in sorrow.

"Please enter and tell us what's on your mind," Giulia demanded.

"May I sit?" he asked. He introduced himself as Hans, nothing more.

"Please."

"Thank you." He slumped into a chair and took a deep breath before beginning. "I learned that one of my soldiers had violated you. When he returned that awful night, he was totally drunk, slurring his words. Eventually I managed to figure out what he was saying and I was horrified. I had thought of you as a little sister. I wanted to help you. That's why I gave you the food."

"Why then did you follow her home to learn where she lived?" Giulia demanded.

"I wanted to watch over her. I have a sister in Germany. She's my only family now. I would have wanted someone to watch over her."

Giulia studied him, puzzled. "Where are your parents?"

"I don't know where they are . . . They may well be dead."

"What do you mean?" Luisa was now becoming involved as she heard more of his story. "Why don't you know where they are?"

His sigh suggested how his heart was broken. "My parents were against the Fascists and they spoke out publicly against them—not the smartest thing in 1935. They acted recklessly... especially since my father was half Jewish, but their consciences wouldn't allow them to be silent."

Giulia and Luisa gasped as one. He looked up at this sound from them. "Yes, that makes me part Jewish."

"But how...?" mother and daughter sputtered in unison.

"How did I end up as a soldier in Hitler's army? A good question. My parents had always acted to protect me... and my sister. At their worst moment when the Aryan laws were promulgated, my parents hatched a devious scheme to protect me and my sister: they signed a statement that my Christian mother had had a liaison with another man—an unquestionable Aryan—so that neither child was even a smidgen Jewish. We were legally Aryan. One of their lifelong friends backed them up with this lie, saying that he was my father as well as my sister's. When I think of the shameful thing my parents had to do to protect me and my sister, I want to hit someone, but the person I want to hit is untouchable."

Luisa and Giulia found their hearts melting for this youth and his family. "You and your family have been through a lot, as we all have," Giulia said. She was almost made speechless in trying to take in all this information.

"I always tried to treat Italians with respect and to help them when I possibly could."

"It's not for us to judge," said Luisa, remembering now what truly was his kindness in giving her the food. She hardly knew what more she could say. Her heart was heavy for him, for herself, for all of them caught in the shameful consequences of this war. Why hadn't the Allies at Anzio moved more quickly? she wondered again.

"We all have much to answer for. At times, I've actually thought about deserting, but I didn't think that would do much good. As a matter of fact, it might have made things worse for you Italians, not to have me on the scene since I was sympathetic to your plight. Sometimes, so that my soldiers wouldn't get suspicious about me, I had to act tough, but that wasn't me. I had such anguish over serving in Hitler's army. It was tearing me apart."

Luisa and Giulia stood by silently. There was so much to say, but they didn't know where to start. Finally, Giulia rose from her chair and said, "Can I make you some coffee from the hoard you so kindly gave us?" She smiled.

The soldier smiled back. "That would be a real pleasure, to have coffee with two lovely ladies." He bowed his head. "I miss my sister very much," he continued, "and hope that she's safe but it's impossible to find out anything. Postal services have fallen apart and we never did have a telephone. So, I'm at a loss."

Giulia made the espresso and, while stirring in the sugar, handed it to him in her best china demitasse cup. The sugar, of course, was the sugar he had given them. He sipped it with pleasure. Even Luisa took pleasure in seeing his pleasure, although she was still unable to erase the image of that other soldier who had violated her. "The best cup of coffee since I've been here. Thank you."

"Hans," Giulia began almost without thinking things through, "would you like to join us for our main meal at noon a week from now? It won't be much—a little polenta, and . . ." Before she could finish her sentence, he accepted her invitation and left.

"Mamma, what have you done? We'll be accused of consorting with the enemy. How could you?"

"I know I acted without thinking. Impetuously even. More from a mother's heart than anything else, but sometimes, Luisa, one must make one's own decisions without worrying about what others will think." With that, Giulia stood up and left the room. Luisa was left with her own thoughts.

MADDIE

Providence, October 1978

Maddie was at another rally. They were interminable. She mingled as best she could but her mind was elsewhere. She was thinking about Pete and Alice among other things, such as her last class and also how her campaign was going. She found it interesting that so many of her students believed that little had changed for women since Artemisia's time. As for her campaign, she had gone into this with full knowledge that she was being used as a "sacrificial lamb" to cover a slot. She was living up to her end of the bargain, doing her best. That was the important thing.

The arrival of Dee interrupted her thoughts. She was on the arm of a man who was one of the party hangers-on. They both looked more proud of themselves than anything else as they strode in. They stopped at the entryway and surveyed the crowd. The man had a barrel chest and a rather beefy face. Ah well, Maddie thought, Dee wanted to hook up with someone and she has, and *he's* probably gained from being connected to her. To each her own, she thought, but she was surprised that Dee hadn't mentioned anything to her about him. Maddie thought that she and Dee were close, but maybe theirs was just a political friendship and not a real friendship. Maddie was still learning. Dee didn't even come over to introduce Maddie to her gentleman "friend."

The next morning, Dee called Maddie. "Hi, Maddie. I wanted to apologize for not introducing you to Paul."

"That's all right, Dee," Maddie said lamely, avoiding any mention of her hurt. Overnight she had thought more about why Dee hadn't introduced her to Paul. He wasn't a player of any political importance and Dee may have been slightly embarrassed by her bald sexual desire for a man so beneath her late husband's stature. The two of them strutting in last night—strutting seemed to be Paul's default posture—was probably, Maddie reasoned, done to save face and deflect any comments—negative ones, anyway.

"It was a huge crowd with lots of other 'people' to see—the 'real' people at any rally," Maddie said.

Dee laughed at Maddie's reference to "people," remembering their laughter at Dee's referring to politicians as the only "real" people and ignoring the rest of the world. "Yeah, sometimes I just get carried away."

"I know what you mean," Maddie said. She couldn't stay mad at Dee for very long. There was something so transparent and honest about her. Maddie chuckled and shortly after, they hung up their phones. More power to her, Maddie thought. Dee needed a man in her life.

Maddie thought about her relationship with Jack. She liked him a lot, but was put off by his great need for a relationship. Maddie wasn't at that place in her life. She needed breathing room. She liked being free from the obligations that relationships bring. She and Jack were at different stages of their lives: she had been married for a decade and a half; Jack had never been married and was eager to settle down now that he was in his late thirties. Besides, his father, who owned a small, successful factory, was pressuring him to go into business with him. He stressed to Jack the vagaries of a life in the arts. Steady work was hard to come by, he instructed. He would tire of giving lessons to beginners.

But business was anathema to Jack. He played classical guitar and gave lessons. He loved his students—even those who had no potential. He loved them just for wanting to make music. He encouraged them all. Oh, well, Maddie thought, time will sort things out. She didn't want to add another worry to her thoughts. The campaign, Pete and Alice were enough for now.

ARTEMISIA

Rome, early 1600s

Father kept his word and brought Tassi to court on the basis of his having lost something, namely my worth to him. I entered the *Sala del Tribunale* almost a year after Tassi had raped me in 1611. The judge, Lord Hieronimo Felicio, was dressed in magnificent scarlet robes. I felt dwarfed by his splendor. I steeled myself for whatever might come. I had waited so long for this day.

First, since I had no standing to take any action—no less bringing someone before the court—my father was called to state why he had brought Tassi to court. Father was not shy about his claim of the loss of my worth.

"Tassi, by his actions, has taken something from me."

"What might that be?" the judge prodded.

"He not only stole one of my daughter's paintings, but he also stole her worth to me, both as an artist and as a father with a marriageable daughter."

"Have you asked Tassi to marry your daughter?"

"Yes, I have. Repeatedly, for the last year but he refuses." Even as my trial started, Father was still trying to get Tassi to marry me. How absurd, I thought. Tassi had made it clear that he had no interest in marrying me.

"Why is that?"

"You will have to ask him," my father said simply.

"You said that Tassi stole a painting from you. Please tell us how you know that."

"After he raped my daughter, he took a painting that she had done from her studio—the studio where he had raped her. My daughter saw him do it," my father fudged. At that time, I was in no condition to notice anything. It was only after I returned to the studio, after the rape, that I noticed that the painting was gone. No one else had been in the studio so it had to be Tassi who had taken it. Besides, when he initially entered my studio to rape me, he kept shouting, 'No more painting, no more painting.' He was in a rage and must have wanted to get revenge for all the accomplished painting I had done. He was mad as well at my friendship with Giorgio. After the encounter in the garden, his hostility towards Giorgio and me was at a fever pitch.

"Who was chaperoning your daughter in the studio?" the judge asked.

"A neighbor woman, named Tuzia, whom I had hired after my wife died when my daughter was twelve. She was Artemisia's usual chaperone. But that day, Tuzia concocted some story about her sister asking her to help take care of her sick child and she left Artemisia in the studio alone."

"We will now hear from Tuzia and her sister." The judge called upon his assistant to bring Tuzia before him.

"Please tell the court why you weren't in the studio as you usually were, on the day in question? May I remind you that you must tell the truth or you will be severely punished."

Tuzia stared at the judge. For a long time, she said nothing. Her eyes shifted left and right, back and forth. She glanced at her sister and made a face.

"Come, come, *Signora*. Let's hear what you have to say. Do not waste our time in useless silence," scolded the judge. Still, Tuzia said nothing. Finally, the judge said, "If you do not speak now, I shall have you put in prison."

Tuzia started to talk in a flood of words coming out of her mouth all at once. It was difficult to follow what she was saying. The judge ordered her to slow down and repeat whatever it was she had said. "I don't have patience for such nonsense. Be careful, *Signora*," he warned.

Tuzia took a deep breath and started over. "Before he came over, Augusto asked me not to go to the studio when he arrived that day."

"By Augusto, do you mean Augusto Tassi?" the judge was losing patience. He drummed his fingers on the table.

"Yes." Tuzia started again. "Augusto Tassi asked me to stay away from her studio on the day of the rape. But I had no idea that was his plan. He was sweet on her; it was easy to see. He would always hang over her and talk in a honeyed voice to her. I thought he wanted to be alone with her, to court her with some pleasurable, agreeable words that all lovers whisper to each other." Tuzia stopped and took a breath.

"Continue," said the judge.

"There's nothing more to tell."

"Isn't there?" prodded the judge.

"Well," Tuzia hesitated and then whispered, while tilting her head toward the judge, "he did give me a little present of a few *lire*, but I thought of it as a present for the chaperoning I had been doing for so many years."

"Most admirable," Lord Hieronimo Felicio said sarcastically.

The judge next called Tuzia's sister. He ascertained that none of the sister's children were sick on the day in question and that she had not asked Tuzia for help.

Next, he called Tassi to testify. The judge asked him to tell the court about that day. Tassi looked around him with a supercilious expression on his face, as if to say that he was above all this inquiry.

"I went to Artemisia Gentileschi's studio as usual to tutor her in the finer aspects of painting. She was hopeless, determined to do things her way—which was all wrong. She rarely concentrated on what I was instructing her to do. Instead, she would lean against me and sigh and then breathe out and ask in that little voice of hers, 'Oh *maestro*, how I wish I could please you—in any way.' Her manner was very provocative. I'm a man, Lord Felicio, but I'm a man of honor and I brushed off her advances as best as I could.

"I was never left alone with Artemisia—her father must have

known what she was like. Tuzia always chaperoned her. I may have given Tuzia a few *lire* for her good work chaperoning Artemisia. For nothing else. I repeat, for nothing else. After all, everyone knows that Orazio Gentileschi is tight with his money and he took advantage of Tuzia's good nature and underpaid her. So, I threw her a couple of *lire*, the poor woman. After all, Lord Felicio, I was well enough off from all my commissions from the bishop and others to do this small kindness for the woman."

Lord Hieronimo Felicio re-called Tuzia. He asked her again if she had been in the studio when Tassi had arrived. He reminded her that she was under an oath to tell the truth. She repeated her earlier testimony. The judge pursued the issue further. "Did the Gentileschi's give you any money to accuse Signor Tassi of engineering your absence from the studio that day?"

Tuzia answered with one word, "No."

"Did Tassi give you money to stay away from the studio that day? Is that why, afterwards, you told Artemisia that your sister had asked you to help her with her sick child?"

"Yes, Lord Felicio. Tassi gave me money to stay away that day. That is the truth." Tuzia dropped her head. "I'm ashamed to admit I lied to Artemisia about why I wasn't in the studio that day."

"*Signor* Tassi. Later on, we'll look into this issue further, but at the moment, your testimony about why you gave Tuzia money is in doubt. What else do you have to say for yourself?"

"I say that this woman is lying. Why would I want to be alone with Artemisia? As far as I was concerned, she was a pest whom I had agreed to tutor, an untalented neophyte. I rue the day that I agreed to Orazio Gentileschi's pleadings. Even then, he was plotting how to bring me down. He was always jealous of my artwork and the many commissions I received. He thought by causing me scandal that he'd get the commissions I had gotten. I did not rape Artemisia Gentileschi."

"Later on, we shall delve into your allegations further as to any proof of what you say. But for now, we shall adjourn until tomorrow."

I was in a rage about Tassi's lies. I needed to calm myself so that when it was my turn to testify, I'd be believable and able to sweep away all his nonsense. I needed to get a good night's sleep so that I'd be at the top of my game. This was not the time to falter.

The next day, Tassio continued his "testimony." "My Lord, she was always with a lot of men. One day I saw her walking in a garden with a slip of a boy, she was that desperate. I have here love letters that she wrote to many men. She was nothing more than a whore, whom her father sold for a loaf of bread."

I didn't know where these letters came from. I didn't even know how to read and write. Father thought it was useless for me—and for girls generally—to be educated. He educated my brothers, who read Ovid, among other great writers, but I was put to the task of grinding his pigments at the age of ten. How used I felt and how lied against I was.

"Please give the letters to the notary to inspect and hold."

Tassi wasn't finished. "She worked as a nude model as well, Lord Felicio, even modeling for her father in the nude. Depraved, she was, and I was supposed to teach her the techniques of the fine arts. Oh, how badly I was used." With that, Tassi appeared to swipe away at a tear in his eye. I was livid.

I was called up next. Tassi told so many lies I didn't know where to begin. I forced myself to be calm and began at the beginning.

"First of all, those purported letters by me couldn't be by me. My father, Orazio Gentileschi, did not believe in educating daughters. I can neither read nor write. My father engaged Signor Tassi to instruct me in various aspects of painting. I complied although I soon discovered that Signor Tassi had little to teach me. Often, he would push up against me when teaching under the guise of looking at the work I was doing at the easel. I ignored such actions.

"On the morning of his rape of me, he arrived at the studio like a wild man. That morning, I might add, was after he saw me walking in a garden with a friend a few days earlier. He had made a scene about my being with Giorgio. Tuzia was there with me. It was one of the few times that I had ever been outside with a friend. Giorgio helped me to look carefully at nature and its wonders so that my paintings would be more accurate.

"The reason Tassi gave Tuzia money was, as she testified, to keep her away from the studio that day. As for these love letters"—I repeated my earlier testimony to be sure it was noted—I spat the words out, "I cannot read or write. My father did not believe in educating girls."

The judge sat back in his chair. "Please re-call Signor Orazio Gentileschi."

"Is it true, Signore, that your daughter could neither read nor write?"

Before Father could answer, Tassi was yelling. "She had someone else write her words down."

"Please be quiet, Signor Tassi. You'll have your chance to speak again, later on, I promise you, about this and other statements being made. Thank you for your cooperation." I saw how Lord Felicio treated Tassi with respect. Everyone was aware that Tassi knew powerful people. My father testified that I neither knew how to read nor how to write. With that, the judge asked Tassi to have the person who "wrote" the letters for me to appear in court tomorrow.

I continued with my testimony. "As I was saying, Signor Tassi entered my studio that morning like a madman. He shouted at me, 'No more painting, no more painting.' He grabbed my palette and brushes from my hands and flung them on the floor. I couldn't figure out why he was yelling those words and doing what he was doing, but there was menace in his words. I grabbed a knife to protect myself and stabbed at him, but they were only superficial wounds. You can still see one of them on his neck. He was too strong for me. I yelled for Tuzia, asking 'Where are you?' but there was no answer to my repeated calls. He flung the knife aside and stuffed a handkerchief into my mouth. He threw me on the floor, onto some paint rags that were lying about, wedged his knee between my legs and raped me."

I stopped for breath. I wanted to say that I was menstruating at the time, but I at first simply said that blood was everywhere. It was very hard to speak of such things. I asked for a glass of water and after I drank it, I continued with a bit more courage. I needed to make the point that I was menstruating.

"I was menstruating at the time. There was blood everywhere. So much blood. I was menstruating," I repeated. I hoped that I didn't have to spell it out for the court: what menstruating woman would try to seduce a man, as Tassi was charging? At that, I lapsed into silence and stared at the floor. The judge stopped the proceedings for the day.

It turned out the proceedings would be stopped for two months. I would have to sit and stew until the proceedings resumed. But little did I know what awaited me. In the meantime, I often overheard the neighborhood gossips, who whispered their conclusions about me. If I were a man, I can't imagine that things would have ended up for me as they did.

LUISA

Rome, June 1944

Luisa was being torn in two. She didn't see things as her mother did. She, not her mother, had been raped. They had two very different views of the situation. She was surprised that her mother was so open to the German and less sympathetic to her own daughter. After all, in a way, it was because of Hans that she had been raped. If he hadn't followed her home in his car with the rapist soldier in the back seat, none of them would have known where she lived and no rape could have occurred. She decided to confront her mother.

"Mamma, I need to talk to you." Luisa explained to her mother how she saw the situation. Her mother responded calmly.

"I'm glad you spoke up, Luisa. I know many things are bothering you, but I didn't want to intrude on your thoughts. I know you're suffering from what happened and I thought it best to say nothing until you spoke. So now that you've spoken, I can tell you what my point of view is.

"You've suffered a terrible blow during this war. War makes everyone victims, in a certain sense. I don't agree that Hans caused your rape. The only person responsible is the man who raped you. Did the third soldier who was in the car rape you? No, it was that one specific soldier who is responsible for his actions. If you say that the responsibility goes back to Hans for following you, could you just as well say that Antonio was responsible for your rape because he sent you out as a courier? Or even that you were responsible for your rape, because you decided to become a courier?"

Luisa stayed silent as she thought through what her mother said.

"I know you're right, Mamma, but I need to blame everyone, the whole world, for what happened to me. I just can't let it go. To forgive Hans, to forgive his fellow soldier is just too much for me right now." She broke down crying.

Giulia took Luisa in her arms. "I know," she soothed, "I know. Forgiveness now isn't possible, but that's not what I'm asking you to do. I'm simply asking you not to blame Hans. Forgiveness will come eventually, but not now. You can't force it. You just need to be open to it, because it'll be of help to you, the person doing the forgiving. The person who assaulted you has no idea—nor does he care probably—if you forgive him or not. Hate just eats *you* up. It doesn't touch him. Your hatred of him doesn't matter one way or another to him. I know forgiveness is hard but that's for another time, not for now. Now you need to look at each person as an individual, responsible for their own actions. You need to heal yourself. Your own strength will get you through this."

Luisa gazed at her mother and marveled at her wisdom. She dried her tears and sat holding her mother's hand.

The week passed and Hans came to the door. He was holding a chicken—a whole chicken—in his hand.

"Oh, Hans," Luisa blurted out in spite of herself, "a chicken. I can't remember when I last saw a chicken. And a whole one at that. Thank you so much. That's so kind of you," she added. Luisa couldn't believe she was saying these words to a German, and a soldier at that.

"Welcome, Hans. I'll broil the chicken and we can eat it after the polenta. I'm drooling already." They all laughed at their undisguised delight. Hans reveled in being with a family. He talked about his sister and told them more about his parents. His father had been a lawyer. Giulia noted that he spoke about his parents in the past tense. She wondered what would become of him once the Allies liberated Rome. German prisoners of war were being sent to America, which had facilities in which to hold them, whereas the European countries had been devastated and therefore were unable to house many war prisoners.

Gossip about the Allies' entry into the city was more and more common and confused. Giulia hoped for all their sakes it would be soon, but still she worried about what would happen to Hans. She couldn't help herself. She was a mother. She would want someone to treat Matteo with the same kindness. Was she really so wrong to have invited Hans to their home?

They began to eat their meal when they heard a key turning in the lock of their apartment door. It opened and in strode Matteo with Antonio. When Antonio saw the German soldier, he immediately reached for his gun and fired at him. Hans had his hand on his gun as well. Antonio's bullet hit Hans's holster and diverted to his shoulder instead of into his chest. Giulia stood up and yelled for all firing to stop. Antonio glared at her. "He's our friend. He has helped us," Giulia said.

"What are you talking about? He's a German soldier. He killed my brother."

"What are *you* talking about, Antonio? He never killed your brother," Giulia said.

"The Germans killed my brother. That's all I know."

"That may well be and I'm so sorry to hear about his death, but Hans had nothing to do with it. He's been stationed in Rome and he has saved us from starvation by giving us food."

Antonio sank to the floor and sobbed. "When will this all end?" he wondered.

A church bell rang out loud and clear. They looked at each other, afraid to understand what that ringing bell meant. Then another church bell added to the music. Finally, all the bells in Rome rang out. The Allies had liberated Rome. For the Romans, the war was over.

ARTIMESIA

Rome, early 1600s

The court had been adjourned for two months when Lord Felicio reconvened proceedings. He called me to repeat my testimony of two months ago, which I did. He found no deviation from my original testimony. Then he asked me to continue with my testimony.

"My father was intent on my marrying for the sake of my honor, but Tassi would have none of it. Father made inquiries and we learned that Signor Tassi was already married. In fact, he had committed incest with his sister-in-law and was found guilty. Furthermore, he hired an assassin to murder his wife. She has been missing for five years.

"Not only wouldn't he marry me, but, out of spite or for some other reason that I'm not acquainted with, he stole one of my paintings."

"What do you have to say for yourself, Signor Tassi?" the judge asked.

"I didn't steal her painting. Her father gave it to me to see if I could find a buyer for it."

"And did you find a buyer for it?"

"No."

"And what about the other charges?"

"I visited Artemisia that day so that she wouldn't be left alone. Tuzia had told me that she wouldn't be able to chaperone because her sister needed her."

"We have already ascertained that Tuzia's sister did not ask her to help with a sick child. We will assume you have nothing to say about your wife's disappearance."

"My wife was a very troubled woman. She left me and I haven't seen her for many years."

"Do you have witnesses to testify that, as you said in this court's first meeting, they wrote these purported love letters for Artemisia?"

Tassi looked down but said nothing. No such witnesses came forward.

With that, Lord Felicio ordered two midwives to examine me in front of the court to ascertain that I was no longer a virgin. They cleared a table and placed me on it. My skirts were hiked up and both the Lord and the notary came to look at me while the midwives examined me. It was humiliating. They testified to the loss of my virginity.

Next, I was put to the *sibille*, the thumbscrews torture, to ascertain if I was telling the truth. The assistant to the Torturer was dressed in a sleeveless leather tunic. Why I remember this detail out of all others, I'll never know.

My fingers were placed at the base within rings. Every time I was asked if I was telling the truth, I answered, "It is the truth," and the thumbscrews were squeezed tighter. They cut through my fingers and they began to bleed. They wouldn't stop bleeding. Was I never to be free from having my blood spilled? I agonized over the harm to my hands that this form of torture was doing. Would I even be able to paint again? I was asked again if I was telling the truth. I answered, "It is the truth." Three times I was asked this and three times the rings were drawn tighter. I feared that if this continued any longer, my fingers would be cut off. Finally, the judge put an end to the thumbscrews, but he never called Tassi forward to see if *he* was telling the truth. Only I was subjected to the *sybille*.

Beside myself with pain, I cried out to Tassi, "This is the ring you gave me and these are your promises." I thrust my mutilated hands towards him.

My testimony and torture counted for something. Tassi's lies were not believed. He was found guilty on all counts—he had to return my painting, which he did—and was banished from Rome for five years. Due to his powerful friends, he never had to leave Rome. He was free to prey on other women.

My hands took a long while to heal but I endured all that suffering and felt vindicated. I began to paint again. The first painting I did after this trial—I poured all my rage into it—was Judith beheading Holofernes. I depicted the blood pouring forth from his wound, just as my blood had been spilled. I pictured Judith as powerful with strong arms and a determined face. She didn't draw back from her deed. I gave her the control that I was not allowed. Her courage was my courage.

EPILOGUE

After the trial, Artemisia's father arranged for her to marry a gentleman from Florence. He wasn't the best partner, but it saved her honor and the honor of the family as the mores of the time demanded. She and her father were not close, but they remained in contact, though there were times when they didn't see each other for almost a decade. Husband and wife eventually separated and lived apart. Given those times, Artemisia's courage in bringing her attacker to court was an extraordinary action. Even today such an action takes extraordinary courage. Artemisia's paintings, acclaimed by critics and the public alike, hang in museums around the world. Tassi's works are rarely remembered or studied.

After the war, Luisa emigrated to America, where she had relatives. She published a slim volume of photographs of rape survivors. Her portraits accomplished what she hoped her portraits would show, the soul of the person. These women's sufferings were evident, but their courage was also visible. She donated her photographs of German soldiers to a Holocaust museum. She never married.

Hans was one of the German prisoners of war sent to America, and one of the few who stayed in America. He never regretted his decision. His surviving sister visited him from time to time. He too never married. He was unable to find out what happened to his parents. He assumed that they, like other opponents of fascism, had died in a concentration camp.

Matteo became a lawyer, mainly representing women who had been raped, and Antonio became his law partner, representing the poor and disenfranchised. They both remained in Rome.

Alice never forgot what had happened to her, but she learned, as best she could, to live with it. Many years after her rape, she and Pete married. They adopted four children. One of their sons went to work for the Providence police department; the other became a priest. Their older daughter married young and she and her husband started their family right away. Their other daughter became a social worker, married and, like her sister, had four children. Alice and Pete adored their eight grandchildren, who loved being part of their large extended family.

Maddie did better than anyone expected in her campaign, but she still lost the election. She was able to put together sufficient funds to rent a small house where rape victims could go for help immediately after their ordeal and receive counseling. Burnout by the volunteer helpers was a problem that led to its demise four years after its founding. Eventually both she and Jack married, but not to each other. Deedee continued to see Paul and remained active in party politics, making sure to see real "people."

The Equal Rights Amendment still has not passed.

ABOUT THE AUTHOR

CAROL BONOMO ALBRIGHT is an American author, editor and educator (having taught at Harvard University Extension School and the University of Rhode Island, Providence); author of three books and editor/co-editor of four anthologies, one of which, *Wild Dreams*, became a Fordham Press best-seller; and *Italian Immigrants Go West*. She attended the Bread Loaf Writers' Conference at Middlebury College and received a Master of Arts in English from Brown University, where she initiated a small press fair.

For 25 years, she was editor in chief of *Italian Americana*, for which Dana Gioia (past chair of the National Endowment for the Arts), at her invitation, agreed to serve as poetry editor. The journal publishes historical articles, as well as fiction, memoirs, and book reviews. She has published numerous articles and book reviews in newspapers, magazines and journals, and received grants from the Danforth Foundation, the National Science Foundation for Medical Education for work using scenes from plays to elucidate the psychosocial issues of medical problems, as well as smaller grants promoting the literary arts.

Hold Up the Head of Holofernes is Ms. Albright's first novel.

ACKNOWLEDGMENTS

Profound thanks are extended to the following for their generous financial support which helped to defray some of this publication's production costs:

Kevin Adams, Max Ahearn, B, Thomas Young Barmore Jr, Melissa Beck, Elena Bertè, Sam Bertram, Gene Blumenreich, Brian R. Boisvert, Michael Bonomo, Tom Bonomo, BR, Jane Brownless, Chris Call, Caterina Leuzzi Castellano, Scott Chiddister, Joel Coblentz, daniel m. cockrell, Andrew Cohn, Christopher T. Cooper, S Costa, Randy and Haley Cox, Parker & Malcolm Curtis, Kathy Curto, AJ Danna, Edward DeFranco, Maryann and Kevin Donovan, Janet Effma, Isaac Ehrlich, Fred Filios, Justin Gallant, GMarkC, B F Gordon Jr, Damian Gordon, Everett Haagsma, Steven Hall, Erik Hemming, Aric Herzog, Fred W Johnson, Dr. Tracy Knight, Stefan Kruger, Raymond Kutch, Kyle, Jean-Jacques Larrea, Leonore, Donna Leuzzi, Josh Mahler, Michael Eric Mancini, Madeline Eboli Masterson, Jim McElroy, Donald McGowan, Michael McGrath, Jack Mearns, Sergio Mendez-Torres, Dr. Melvin "Steve" Mesophagus, Judy Mintz, Marjorie Montgomery, Spencer F Montgomery, Gregory Moses, Scott Murphy, Matt "DevilBoy" Murray, Michael O'Shaughnessy, Christine Palamidessi, Michael Palma, Andrew Pearson, John E Piazza, Bob Plourde, Pedro Ponce, Robert Price, Kate R, Judith Redding, Patrick M Regner, Heidi Reid, Debbie and Allan Roth, Owen Rowe, -S, George Salis (www.TheCollidescope.com), Kristen Scanlan,

Yvonne Solomon, Nicolaus C. Stengl, K. L. Stokes, Supporter,
Michelle and Perry Swenson, Nondas Hurst Voll, Paulie Wenger,
Christopher Wheeling, Isaiah Whisner, Charles Wilkins,
T. R. Wolfe, Sara Zeglin, The Zemenides Family, and Anonymous

www.ingramcontent.com/pod-product-compliance
Lightning Source LLC
LaVergne TN
LVHW031606060526
838201LV00063B/4753